I0674466

Santa Fe Sunrise

Tanya Stowe

Santa Fe Sunrise

COPYRIGHT 2015 by Tanya Stowe

Contact Information: titleadmin@pelicanbookgroup.com

All scripture quotations, unless otherwise indicated, are taken from the Holy Bible, New International Version(R), NIV(R), Copyright 1973, 1978, 1984, 2011 by Biblica, Inc.™ Used by permission of Zondervan. All rights reserved worldwide. www.zondervan.com

Cover Art by *Nicola Martinez*

White Rose Publishing, a division of Pelican Ventures, LLC
www.pelicanbookgroup.com PO Box 1738 *Aztec, NM * 87410

White Rose Publishing Circle and Rosebud logo is a trademark of Pelican Ventures, LLC

Publishing History
First White Rose Edition, 2015
Electronic Edition ISBN 978-1-61116-502-9
Paperback Edition ISBN 978-1-61116-535-7
Published in the United States of America

Dedication

To my Mom, who inspired me with stories of Taos.

What People are Saying

Tender Touch

I loved this book, and can say in all honesty that it is one of the best I've read in the past year...and possibly longer. Stirring and thought-provoking, it also contains a sprinkle of humor and a dusting of fun. Truly inspired writing! ~ Delia Latham

1

Brett Fraser couldn't move his neck. He'd caught a few hours' sleep hunkered into the crevice between his car seat and the door. His right hand throbbed with tiny needles as the circulation came back, and his knee, wrapped around the gearshift, wouldn't unbend even after he sat up.

As soon as I get off this back road and locate Santa Fe, I'm going to find a nice hotel, a shower and a king-sized bed.

Sleeping in his car had definitely lost its charm. After six months of a self-imposed sabbatical touring the great Southwest, he was ready for some creature comforts.

One thing for sure, he'd seen some spectacular country. The Grand Canyon with its sheer drop-offs and hidden valleys. Lake Powell's amazing mixture of colors—blue, green and a thousand variations of rust. Canyon de Chelly, the Navajos' sacred place, with its smooth, sheer walls of swirling sandstone and cliff dwellings. Absolutely unbelievable.

He might not know where or how he fit into it, but one thing was clear, God had a plan. Anyone who'd witnessed these spectacular sights had to recognize the Master Artist at work.

Case in point: the sunrise in front of him.

In Arizona, fire burned the skies during sunrise and sunset. Bright golden light and fireballs of orange and gold lit the horizon. But here, in New Mexico, the colors were softer, more subtle. Above the dark ridge, the horizon was streaked as if by a paintbrush with bands of subtle gray blending into purple, then mauve, and finally pink.

Amazing.

Brett sat up straighter, peering closely.

A head appeared behind the ridge, coming over. When the runner reached the top, she turned and ran along the slender path with a smooth stride. A long ponytail swung behind her, giving her a graceful rhythm, almost like a dancer swaying from side to side. Completely shadowed with the pastel sunrise behind, her curvy figure stood out in dark relief.

Brett shoved the fast-food bags off the seat beside him, searching for his phone. If he could just get a snap of her with both feet off the ground, the pastel horizon showing beneath her...

"Come on, come on." The password lock took forever, and the camera even longer to open. At last he had the lens focused on the woman. He watched the mesmerizing rhythm of her movements, waiting for just the right moment.

Suddenly, the runner stumbled and disappeared from the lens. Brett lowered the phone just in time to see a dark running suit rolling down the sand-colored hill.

He threw his cell to the seat and bolted from the car, leaving the door open and the keys in the ignition. As he skidded down the gravel side of the road, his car set up an outraged beep. Ignoring the incessant sound, he leapt over a small tumbleweed and kept running.

Brett topped a small rise. The runner sat at the bottom of a culvert just below the ridge. One dark running shoe lay off to the side, and the woman was bent over, gripping her right ankle.

"Are you all right?"

The injured woman screamed and nearly bounced off the ground.

"Where in the world did you come from?" Her voice was low and a bit husky...a bedroom kind of voice.

Brett purposely put that thought behind him as he knelt beside her. "I'm parked on the road down there. I saw you trip."

"My shoelace broke." She picked up the offending article and tossed it away with a disgusted flick of her wrist. "Just snapped. My shoe came loose and almost fell off. Of course, it had to happen right while I was running The Rope."

"The Rope?"

Her chin nudged up. "That's what I call that ridge. It's narrow and has drop offs on both sides. Sometimes, when the wind blows, it feels as if I'm crossing a swaying rope bridge. I run over it every day and never had a problem...until this." She pushed the shoe further away.

Brett picked it up and examined the broken lace's smooth edges. Something about it bothered him but at that moment, the lovely runner gave a soft moan and rocked over her injured ankle again.

"Mind if I take a look?"

She nodded, her teeth clenched in pain.

Brett eased back the short sock. Purple bruising already showed around the rapidly swelling ankle. "This needs ice and maybe even a doctor. Let's get you back to my car."

"I can't stand on it. I already tried."

"All right. Just let me do the work." He rose to his

feet, picked up the shoe, and tucked it in his coat pocket. The thick tread barely fit, but he wiggled it in as best he could. Then he braced his feet. "Just let me lift you. Don't put any weight on your foot, OK?"

She nodded and Brett grasped her upper arms. She got her good leg beneath her and stood to her full height with surprising speed, considering her injury. On the ridge she'd seemed much taller but in reality, she couldn't have been more two or three inches over five feet.

Up close, her olive skin was pale and had a soft sheen—not from running, but pain. Full pink lips were clenched tight, and when she leaned into Brett for better balance, something sweet and exotic wafted up from her black hair.

Get a grip, Fraser. She's in pain.

That didn't stop him from wishing she'd look up so he could see the color of her eyes. But a little moan of pain banished even that thought from his mind. He gripped her arms to steady her.

"Gravity is sending all the blood straight to the injury. Give it a second and the pain will ease up a bit. When it does, just nod and we'll get moving."

"OK." A near whimper. But the woman was a trooper. After just a few minutes she nodded.

He looped her right arm over his shoulder and gripped her waist. "Your job is to keep off that ankle no matter what, got it? Let me do all the work. You just keep your other leg balanced."

She nodded again and Brett started up the hill. Her petite frame couldn't match his five-eleven one, so he ended up carrying her most of the way up. At the top, he had to pause and catch his breath before making their way down the other side.

Half an hour later, they finally reached the road. Brett climbed the gravel side of the highway with his limp, exhausted runner cradled in his arms and set her on the dust-covered fender of his car.

"Rest here for a moment."

She leaned to her side, trying to pull her ankle up.

"When we get inside," Brett said between breaths, "prop it up on the dash. Elevating it will relieve some of the pain."

"How do you know so much about injured ankles?"

Brett bent over to stretch his taut back muscles. "My best friend was in a car crash. I helped out with the recuperation therapy." Straightening, he opened the passenger door. The scent of old French fries wafted out along with other stale odors. The injured woman looked at the hardened fries scattered across the seat, then leaned forward, openly gaping at his clothes, thrown helter-skelter over the back.

"Are you...living in your car?"

"Not exactly. I prefer to call this experience a sabbatical."

She straightened and pulled a cellphone out of her jacket pocket. "I—I think I'll call my mother and let her know what's happened."

Brett chuckled. "Good idea. Call her and let her know a man named Brett Fraser will be taking you to the doctor in a sports car." He recited the license plate and model of his car.

She paused, the phone halfway to her ear. "Brett Fraser? *The* Brett Fraser, director of the Fallon School of Art?"

A solid ball of disappointment slid straight down Brett's throat and settled in his stomach. "Ex-director.

I'm the ex-director." He pulled her shoe out of his pocket and tossed it to the back.

"That's right. You resigned after some sort of scandal."

Brett glanced back at the beautiful horizon, now washed white by bright sunlight. "It's good to know my life in Sedona was important enough to make the headlines in Santa Fe."

"Not the headlines." She looked up and directly into his eyes.

Brown. Her eyes were the darkest, richest chocolate he'd ever seen. Rimmed with long black lashes, they rivaled anything he'd viewed in a painting.

"I own a gallery," she said. "Art is my business. To me, the Fallon school opening so close to home was big news."

"I see. And do I get to know your name?"

"Rafaela."

Figured. Even her name was exotic and beautiful.

"Well, Rafaela, now that you know all about me and my past, am I safe enough to take you to the doctor?"

Those lovely full lips thinned into another grimace of pain before she nodded. "Yes, please."

~*~

"Now, Rafaela, you absolutely must rest and keep all strain off this ankle."

She nodded dutifully. Doctor Aguilar had been her doctor most of her life so he knew her very well. She wasn't at all surprised when he raised a finger and pointed it directly at her nose.

"I mean it, young lady. Absolutely no weight. The X-rays show nothing broken, but tissue damage can be even worse. If you don't stay off it, you can turn a four-week recuperation into two months or longer."

Rafaela promised and crossed her heart.

The doctor *hmphed* with disbelief. "Well, just in case, I'll be calling your mother with the same instructions." The white-haired man turned away. "Now, I'm writing a prescription for pain. I want you to sleep today. It's still the best treatment for injuries. But I'm only prescribing enough pills for today and tomorrow. I don't want you taking these, thinking they'll help you to go back to work. No work for at least a week."

Rafaela stifled the hasty words on her lips. She didn't need to tell Dr. Aguilar that she had to work. He knew—almost everyone knew—how badly Rafaela needed the money. The de Silva Gallery was the only thing keeping her family afloat.

Her mother, Lucia, tried to help out by teaching dance lessons at their home. But Mama had scaled back even those efforts after Sofia's illness had grown worse.

In fact, they'd almost lost Rafaela's younger sister after her latest bout with anorexia.

Rafaela squeezed her eyes shut as the image of more hospital bills floated through her mind. Now she could add hers to Sofia's growing pile.

"No need to buy crutches," Dr. Aguilar said, almost as if reading her thoughts. "I have a pair I keep in the office. They won't be missed in the short three to four weeks you'll be on them, right?" The older man peered at her over the rim of his glasses, waiting for the appropriate response.

Rafaela couldn't stop the smile that slipped over

her lips. "Absolutely, Doctor. Three or four weeks maximum."

"Good." He ripped the prescription paper off the tablet and handed it to her. "Now you wait right there while I go get those crutches and your young man."

"He's not…"

The doctor was gone before she could explain that Brett Fraser wasn't her young man. Not that deep down, in some dark hidden part of her, Rafaela didn't wish it might be so. Something utterly charming about Brett Fraser gave him an irresistible appeal. Not just his good looks either, although he had those in abundance.

Brown hair parted to one side with a tendency to fall slightly forward. Light-colored eyes. Were they brown or green? She couldn't remember. Even the shadow of three or more days' worth of whiskers couldn't hide his fine features.

Maybe it was the beard that gave him that devil-may-care impression. No, that was definitely his fined-tuned wry humor. If she hadn't been in pain, she would have laughed at some of his clever little remarks.

A wave of dizziness forced Rafaela to lean back on the examining table. The shot Dr. Aguilar had given her for pain was definitely having an impact—in more ways than one. Rafaela never, ever mooned or daydreamed over a man. She didn't have time for relationships and certainly wasn't the type to fantasize over a strong jaw and chin…even if the chin did have a very nice little cleft.

She giggled out loud. OK. So what if Brett Fraser was going to get a relaxed—make that a very relaxed—version of the real Rafaela? Tomorrow, he'd be on his way…gone from her life, and she could get back to the business of being cold, shut down, and aloof. *Where in the world did that come from?* She took several deep, cleansing breaths. They helped to clear her head, but that didn't stop her from grinning like a fool when Brett walked in.

"Hey, how are you feeling?" His hazel eyes—yes, definitely hazel—were wide and shadowed with concern.

"I'm feeling fine now that the shot's starting to work."

"Ahhh, a shot." A smile slid into place. "So you're feeling no pain."

"Nope. No pain." She giggled.

Brett chuckled with her.

"Well, it won't last long." Dr. Aguilar stepped up behind Brett. "So the sooner we get these crutches adjusted and you on your way, the better."

As soon as the crutches fit Rafaela's short arms, the doctor settled her in a wheelchair and pointed Brett towards the door. "It's a long way to her ranch so you'd better get started."

Brett turned her around while Rafaela thanked the doctor and his nurse.

Release papers and receipts clutched in her hand, she turned back just in time to see a tall, broad-shouldered man enter the clinic.

"*Tío!* What are you doing here?" Rafaela sagged. "Oh never mind, I know. My mother called you, didn't she?"

"Of course she did. Fortunately, she caught me between meetings while my phone was still on."

"Well, even more fortunately, you can head right back to those meetings." Rafaela gestured to her wrapped ankle. "As you can see, it's just a sprain. I'm going to follow the doctor's orders and rest. Oh, this is Brett Fraser. He found me, and now he's offered to finish the job and drive me home."

Her uncle's little jolt of surprise caught her off guard. Did he recognize Brett's name, too? Or was the drug still pushing her imagination into overdrive? That must have been the case because her uncle said nothing, only extended his hand toward Brett for a shake.

"Thank you, Mr. Fraser. We truly appreciate your help, but I'll take over now."

In her condition, Rafaela couldn't stop the impulsive giggle that slipped out. "Tío, you're acting like an over-protective father. Everything's fine, truly fine."

"She's right, Mr. ..."

"Pomeroy. Aaron Pomeroy."

"Mr. Pomeroy, I'm on vacation. I have nothing planned for the rest of the day, and you've already said you have meetings. I'll be more than happy to take Rafaela home."

"Thank you, Mr. Fraser, but no meeting is more important to me than Rafaela's welfare. Besides, her mother would never let me hear the end of it if I let her go home with a perfect stranger."

With that, Tío pulled the wheelchair forward, out of Brett's hands, and pushed it toward the door.

Brett hurried ahead to hold the door open as her uncle pushed her out.

Tío's car was parked right in front of the clinic, the motor running.

How like Tío, thinking the laws don't apply to him. Rafaela smiled at her own thoughts. In truth, rules and regulations usually didn't apply to a man as important as her adopted uncle.

He stopped the wheelchair, lifted Rafaela into the comfortable passenger seat, and pushed the chair back toward Brett. "If you wouldn't mind taking that back inside, I'd appreciate it. I want to get Rafaela home as quickly as possible." He pulled out a business card and handed it to Brett. "Here's my number if you'd like to contact me about her condition. We can't thank you enough for all your help. Her mother is most grateful. If you're staying long, maybe I can offer you dinner. It's the least I can do."

As he shut her car door, Rafaela murmured a thank you and waved at her handsome rescuer.

Tío came around, slid into the driver's seat beside her, and punched the car into gear.

Rafaela looked back to see a rather forlorn-looking Brett still standing on the curb.

2

Brett stretched to his full length in the king-sized bed. Crisp sheets and a clean smell wrapped around him. Definitely much better than yesterday morning.

He'd found a five-star hotel close to downtown, right next to an interesting little chapel he wanted to check out. But more importantly, the hotel was located just a few blocks from Santa Fe's central plaza. Last night, as he glanced through the hotel's welcome brochure, he'd seen an advertisement for the de Silva Gallery, situated right on the plaza.

As soon as he enjoyed a hot shower, a sit-down breakfast complete with a waitress, and cleaned out his car, he was going to check on his lovely little runner. And he had no intention of going through her high-handed uncle, Aaron Pomeroy.

Granted, Brett was a stranger in Santa Fe. He could understand Rafaela's family might have concerns. But her uncle had been just plain rude, and her mother sounded like a dragon lady with her mama claws out. If they'd intended to put him off, they'd missed the mark, only succeeding in creating more mystery. Rafaela was a capable, competent young woman. So why were they so overprotective?

No wonder she took long runs in the back of beyond. She likely needed every escape she could find. And Brett was just the man to provide one.

Of course, dark brown eyes and a desire to see her

with her hair down had nothing to do with it. He was a man on a rescue mission. Grinning, he flipped back the covers and headed for the shower.

~*~

The hot August sun turned Brett's dark shirt into a heating pad. Yesterday, the tail end of a storm had brought cooler temperatures, but today the summer temps were back with a vengeance. Sweat trickled down between his shoulder blades as he stood in the center plaza of downtown Santa Fe.

Roads and storefronts surrounded the small park on four sides. Behind Brett, the Palace of the Governors covered an entire block. Built in the seventeenth century, the adobe building had once been Spain's seat of government for the American Southwest. Now, Native Americans displayed their crafts and handmade jewelry on colorful woven blankets spread beneath the palace's massive covered portico.

Cleaning out his car had taken longer than he'd anticipated. He'd stacked the boxes from his car in his hotel room, where he'd sorted a month's worth of dirty clothes and sent them to the hotel laundry. Finding a place to have his car washed inside and out ate up another hour.

All his extra efforts and time had paid off. Buried in the pile of soiled laundry, he'd found the excuse he needed to see Rafaela again. He'd forgotten her very new, very expensive running shoe. Of course he had to return it. Ready to storm the castle and free the princess, he flipped the shoe in the air, caught it and crossed the street.

When Rafaela first mentioned her gallery, the

name had struck a bell. While preparing to open the Fallon School of Art, Brett had researched the larger cities and art centers of the Southwest. Santa Fe definitely fit the bill as a cultural center.

Artists and musicians flocked to the quaint capital of New Mexico with its Pueblo architecture, unique fashion flair, and desert mountain atmosphere. Nestled in the surrounding hills was the spectacular open-air Santa Fe Opera House. Live theatre, music and food festivals filled the social calendar, and some of the finest galleries in the States could be found on these streets.

Brett didn't remember exactly why the de Silva Gallery had stood out from the crowd, but he definitely remembered the name. He spotted the gallery directly in front of him, waited for the traffic to clear, and crossed.

A small, moveable display wall, painted gray, stood prominently in the gallery's floor-to-ground window. Centered on the wall, a painting with bright-blue jagged lines, yellow suns, and orange lizards caught his eye. The colors exploded on the neutral backdrop. Not far away, a wood carving of a horse reared on a deep purple pedestal. Beyond that, glass shelves with a soft, pale-pink backlight showcased artfully arranged pottery pieces in stark black.

Tastefully done. The lighting, the moveable walls, and the open space, provided tremendous visual appeal. A real class act, the de Silva Gallery.

Brett's appreciative gaze took in the spectacular sunrise colors he had witnessed yesterday morning.

Did Rafaela use them because they worked or because they reminded her of her majestic morning runs? Was she caught in the spell of this land of enchantment, too?

Brett anticipated a pleasurable search for those answers. Pulling the door open, he stepped inside. Flamingo music echoed softly over the air, bringing back not-so-pleasant memories of his recent experiences. That tune was almost certainly the work of Alexander Summers. *Great! Just what I need right now. A reminder of how badly I failed.*

"Can I help you?"

Busy cataloging the mistakes Summers's music jolted from his memory, Brett didn't notice the woman's approach. Seeing her rendered him momentarily speechless.

Talk about beautiful. Tall. Ultra slender. Black hair shot through with white. On anyone else, the silver streaks might have been unattractive but on this woman, with her nearly seamless skin, they were perfect. She wore a long, dark-blue, print skirt with a matching top. Around her neck rested a spectacular, shiny, squash-blossom necklace with a matching bracelet on her wrist. A concho belt nestled over slim hips. She studied him with dark, liquid eyes. Something about those eyes…

"I'm sorry." He'd been staring. Great way to make an impression. He'd clearly been away from polite society too long. "I'm Brett Fraser."

"Oh, Mr. Fraser." The woman crossed the space and cupped his hands with hers.

A little surprised, he gripped Rafaela's running shoe tighter.

"I'm so glad you came." Her husky tones soothed something in Brett's soul. "I was very annoyed with Aaron when he told me he didn't get a number where we could reach you. I'm Lucia de Silva, Rafaela's mother."

So much for his dragon-lady concept. This woman epitomized gentility…warm, vibrant and lovely.

"Well, Rafaela's uncle did offer to buy me dinner." Brett's tone reflected just how insincere he believed the offer to have been.

A frown clouded her features. "You must forgive Aaron. He's very…protective. You see, he's Rafaela's adopted uncle, my husband's lifelong friend. Ever since Rafael passed away, Aaron feels we are *his* responsibility. Sometimes I think it's an obligation that causes him more difficulty than he likes to admit."

"Rafaela's father…your husband passed away?"

"Yes, almost four years ago now, from kidney failure."

"I'm sorry for your loss."

"Thank you. It's been…difficult." Her features clouded even more, and Brett wondered what thoughts swam behind those dark brown eyes—eyes that resembled her daughter's.

Brett gestured with the shoe to the painting beside them. "Your gallery is very impressive. Have you run it since your husband's passing?"

She smiled. "No. This is all Rafaela's inspiration. Since she took over, it's prospered. I help out when I can. But not as often as I'd like." She gave a little shake of her head. "This injury couldn't have happened at a worse time. Rafaela's assistant, Jan, just left for a week's holiday."

"Well, it's fortunate you could be here today."

"Yes, this will work for a while. But my daughter, Sofia, is very ill. I can't be away from home for long."

Rafaela had her hands full. A gallery, a widowed mother, an unhealthy sister and a shoelace that appeared to have been cut three quarters of the way through.

Something had struck Brett as odd when he'd first picked up the shoe yesterday. Why had the lace broken on a near-perfect, almost brand new piece of footwear? He'd assumed a faulty eyelet had worn down the lace. But this morning, upon examining the shoe more closely, he found a neat edge on most of the shoelace. Only one corner showed fraying and shredding.

Now he wondered why anyone would want to cut halfway through Rafaela's shoelace. Any reasonable person would know such an act might cause the lace to break and possibly cause her injury.

A lot of responsibility rested on Rafaela's petite shoulders. Did someone want to increase that pressure, or worse, prevent her from meeting her obligations? Her injury seemed certain to cause serious financial problems, given the hospital visit combined with her inability to tend the gallery. But who could possibly want to do that?

No one. People cared about Rafaela, from her overprotective uncle to her fatherly doctor. She seemed to have a community of loved ones, people who could and would help her—not hurt her.

Brett gave himself a mental shake. His recent experiences in Sedona had him imagining conspiracies and danger around every corner. This cross-country trip had been intended to erase those images and feelings. Now, with his first venture back into civilized company, he'd fallen right back into the pattern. *Enough, Fraser. Drop it!* With that resolution, he gave the shoe a little flip in the air.

"Is there a reason you're carrying that piece of my daughter's wardrobe, Mr. Fraser?" The humorous note in Lucia's voice made him grin.

"Yes. I was hoping to pay her a visit so I could return it."

Lucia de Silva gave him a slightly stunning, knowing smile. "Oh, but we can do much better than that. You must join us for dinner at our rancho."

~*~

Brett notched up the speed on his car as he reached a long stretch of road on the way to the de Silva ranch, located five or six miles out of town. Another thing he'd found hidden in the pile in his back seat was his GPS, thrown there when he'd first begun this trip. He was determined to go where the Lord led him, an attitude far different than the one he brought along when he first came out west. In fact, he hadn't updated to a newer GPS because the old one contained all of his favorite locations and spots on the East Coast. He'd had every intention of returning as soon as possible. He never planned on falling in love with this part of the country.

But he had. As the road curved up into the gentle, piñon covered hills, he rolled down the windows. The scent of dry land and pine flowed in, that curious blend unique to the southern Rockies.

Santa Fe nestled on the edge of the Sangre de Cristo Mountains, the last outpost of the majestic Rockies before the land flowed into the flat desert. This area was nature's melding point. Hot days and cool nights. Snow in winter. Cactus and scrub oak.

A certain human melding existed here, as well. Native American and Mexican culture. New Age artists and cowboys. All of them clashing together in a flavor so distinct, it fascinated Brett. Even if he hadn't encountered the equally fascinating Rafaela de Silva, he would have been happy to spend more time in Santa Fe.

He was almost sorry when he came to the large adobe arch marked "de Silva" at the top in huge letters. He turned onto a dirt road that disappeared into distant rolling hills at least a mile away. The de Silva's property must cover a lot of acreage because the house was nowhere in sight. Brett's car climbed up and over gentle dips until the road spilled into an open valley. He saw a small, flat mesa in the distance, but right in the middle of the valley sat a sprawling hacienda surrounded by an adobe wall.

Brett pulled his car to a stop in the center of a wide horseshoe driveway. A pathway led to a smaller adobe arch with slightly tilted wooden gates propped open. Outside the gates, a wooden wheel leaned against a rock, and an artful display of cacti lent a bit of charm, but weeds and grass poked through and cluttered the image.

The musical tinkle of falling water caught his attention the moment he stepped out of the car. After grabbing Rafaela's shoe from the back, he walked through the arch. Directly in front of him, a Spanish-style fountain created a welcoming entry piece. Water flowed from a flower-like upper pedestal and tinkled down onto the blue-and-white tiles of the basin with a melodic splash. On the other side of the fountain, the U-shaped house front formed a sheltered courtyard.

Rafaela sat on the rust-colored pad of a wrought-iron chaise longue. A smaller pillow of the same bright, orangey hues propped up her knee and ankle. Beside her, a long, wrought-iron table held a stack of papers and a pen.

To Brett's disappointment, Rafaela's hair did not spill around her shoulders. Instead, she had piled it on top of her head in an artful mess with tendrils escaping here and there. She was without make-up. Her dark eyelashes stood out on cheeks that looked less pale, more golden. She wore a brown sundress with tiny pink embroidered flowers. Bright red toenails peeked out from the long lengths of her dress, and she looked sweet, innocent, and fresh. The only thing missing when he greeted her was a smile.

"You look as if you're feeling much better."

She gave a little shrug to one shoulder. "As well as can be expected. Not too much pain today."

"I hope you're following the doctor's R.I.C.E. instructions."

"Rest. Ice. Compression. Elevation. Just what the doctor ordered." She pointed to the pillows beneath her foot and lifted her skirt just enough to show him an ice pack wrapped around her ankle.

He gestured to the paperwork beside her. "I was thinking more of the 'rest' part."

She flipped the stack over, but not before Brett saw the letterhead: Saint Joseph's Hospital.

"A little bit of paperwork won't tire me out."

But stress will. Their meeting had already started off slow. He wasn't about to add to the awkwardness by probing into an area she obviously didn't want to discuss.

"Besides I stopped working a while ago, when I first heard your car come over the hill."

"You heard that far away?"

"This valley amplifies everything. Sound travels a long way out here."

Brett nodded and held up her shoe.

"Ah, the culprit." She took it from him, shaking her head all the while. "I've used this brand for years. I thought I could count on them." She fingered the offending shoelace. "I guess even the best mess up once in a while."

Brett kept silent again. If she didn't attach any significance to the shoelace, neither would he.

"Please, have a seat." She tossed the shoe to an empty chair beside her.

Brett took the one on the other side of a low table. As he settled in, Rafaela carefully kept her eyes averted. Her coolness was not Brett's imagination. She wasn't comfortable and didn't seem happy to have him here.

"This valley, is it all part of your family's ranch?"

She laughed. Not a good laugh, one with a wry, almost cynical tone. "It's not really a ranch, not anymore. When my grandfather was alive, he ran almost three thousand head of cattle. Once my dad took over, he sold them all. Ranching wasn't his thing. He was a *painter*." The word sounded harsh, almost derogatory.

"He wasn't a very good artist?"

"Actually, he was a great artist. Just a lousy businessman. My father had only two loves—his work and his family. Everything else took little to no place in his attention. So when he passed, he left us with exactly two things…wonderful memories of a loving dad and a mountain of debt." Almost immediately, she closed her eyes. "I'm so sorry. You didn't need to hear that." For the first time since he'd arrived, she met his gaze and a genuine smile flitted across her lips. "What is it about you that brings out such strange behavior in me? Yesterday you saw a silly side. Today, I'm maudlin. I promise you, Brett, you are not seeing the real me."

He captured her sincere gaze with his own. "Well then, I hope you'll give me the chance to get to know the real you because what I've seen so far, I like. A lot."

3

Her mother stepped out of the French doors leading into the kitchen and grasped Brett's arms as if he were a long-lost friend. "I thought I heard Rafaela speaking to someone."

Her familiarity made Rafaela uncomfortable, especially after what Brett had just said.

The attraction had been there, right from the beginning, certainly. But she wasn't prepared for the heart-pounding, finger-tingling response that flared to life inside her at his quiet declaration. Even now, a flush warmed her cheeks.

Could her mother and Brett see how flustered she'd become? Was she so desperate for male attention that she was flopping like a fish on land at the first man to show an interest in her in months...maybe years?

She couldn't remember the last time she'd had a date. Focused on taking care of her family, most of her relationships were centered on her business. At least they had been in her mind. Now that she thought of it, a few of her associates had attempted to get to know her, but she'd been so absorbed with making her family financially secure, she hadn't had time for them.

Truthfully, Brett was the first man to interest her in a long, long time. And that made his visit to her home even more difficult. What would he think about the dilapidated condition of her house? She loved it beyond words, and that was why she clung to it so desperately, but most people wouldn't understand. They'd only see the chipped adobe, broken tiles, and warped wood.

And what would Brett think of Sofia? Would he be kind to her or shocked when he saw her? If he drew attention to her little sister's condition, Sofia would grow nervous and hide in the deep recesses of the house. His visit might even set her recovery back.

Rafaela couldn't understand why her mother had been so quick to invite this near-stranger into their home.

"Your home is—"

Brett's words jolted Rafaela out of her thoughts. "In need of much repair," she finished for him.

He smiled and shook his head. "I was going to say impressive."

"The ranch has been in my husband's family for generations. It was one of the first ranchos in all of New Mexico. Back in the day, Rancho de Silva provided supplies for travelers on the Santa Fe Trail. Our home has a very rich history but Rafaela is right. It needs much repair."

Repairs I can't possibly make. Not to mention back taxes that must be paid in October.

Brett's gaze focused on the arched double doors of the main entrance. "But what a labor of love."

Spoken like someone who has the money and the skills to make those kinds of repairs. Rafaela didn't say the words out loud but what she did say had a definite ring of cynicism. "How interesting that you'd say that, given the Fallons' choice of design for their new school."

Brett smiled and studied her across the table. "So

you read about that battle. Seems to me, you're more than a little interested in the Fallon program, even though it's so far from your home."

Rafaela dared not tell him the other reason she'd researched the school. That hidden thought made it even more difficult to endure his pointed stare.

"What battle is that?" Her mother seemed oblivious to Rafaela's fidgeting.

"Daniel Fallon chose a very modern design for the school building," Brett explained. "Environmentally designed glass walls, steeply pitched roofs, uncommon building materials. Many felt he should have chosen a more traditional Pueblo design for such a monumental project. In spite of the fact that Daniel Fallon made his fortune buying and selling antiquities, he felt it was important to create a benchmark, a look at the future. So he chose a design by a budding young architect."

"Considering the school is for gifted young artists, it sounds to me like a perfect choice."

"I agree, and if you'd seen the building, you would too."

Rafaela couldn't say more without sounding petty or unreasonable. Besides she was anxious to direct the conversation away from the topic of budding young artists.

"Mama, could I have something to drink?"

"Of course. I'm sorry; I should already have offered our guest some refreshment." Her mother directed her voice inside. "Sofia, would you bring out the iced tea?" She smiled at Brett. "My other daughter has been helping me prepare dinner."

"I hope you didn't go to a lot of trouble just for me. You did put in a full day of work," Brett said.

Her mother laughed. "It's no trouble. I love

cooking, and with Sofia acting as my sous chef, we can accomplish great things. I hope you like pork *carnitas*."

"I have no idea what it is, but it sounds wonderful."

"Carnitas means little meats, pieces of pork roasted and seasoned. We can eat it plain or with tortillas."

Her mother and Brett continued to talk, but Rafaela tensed as her younger sister moved out of the shadows of the kitchen carrying a tray laden with a pitcher of tea and glasses full of ice. Sofia's slender arms scarcely seemed strong enough to carry the heavy load, and the concentration on her features assured Rafaela that the task was almost too much for her frail little sister.

Rafaela's heart ached. Sofia and their father had been close. His death, when Sofia was only ten, left her with deep-seated fears and anxiety. For a number of years, she was able to keep a slender control over her constant nightmares and imagination. But when she reached puberty, hormones amplified those issues. Sofia then sought to control her life through her diet and stopped eating.

Now, as a teenager, she weighed less than eighty pounds and had suffered serious bouts of malnutrition and dehydration. In fact, she'd only recently been discharged from the hospital. Strange lights and noises, she claimed, had kept her awake for weeks. Desperate to rest, she'd taken over-the-counter sleeping pills. Her weakened state had caused serious side effects and she'd been admitted for several days.

Rafaela's only comfort lay in the fact that, as far as they knew, the incident had not been a suicide attempt. Sofia had taken the appropriate dosage of the pills. Her body simply wasn't strong enough to handle it.

Now she struggled with the tray, the task complicated by the floppy sleeves of a heavy cable knit sweater that Rafaela knew Sofia wore, along with baggy pants, to conceal her emaciated frame. Acne, brought on by poor nutrition, pitted her face. With gaunt cheeks and dark-circled eyes, she barely resembled the happy, healthy child she'd once been. Even Sofia's hair, once so long and lovely, had suffered. Discouraged by the limp tresses, Sofia had pulled them into a ponytail and cut off the length with scissors. Now the loose ends flopped around her face, hiding her eyes.

Worried about his reaction to her sister's condition, Rafaela's swung her gaze to Brett. If he had a response, he hid it well as Sofia approached and placed the tray on the table.

"Mr. Fraser, this is my daughter Sofia."

"Hello, Sofia, it's a pleasure to meet you."

Sofia mumbled a greeting without meeting his gaze. "If it's OK, Mama, I'd like to go paint until dinner." Her words were just louder than a murmur.

"Of course, we'll call you when it's time."

Sofia spun and hurried away.

"She's a painter, like her father?" Brett asked after Sofia had scooted out of sight.

"Yes, and she's actually very good. Maybe even better than my husband." Rafaela's mother smiled, something soft and sad in her eyes.

The last thing Rafaela wanted was her mother and Brett discussing her sister's artistic abilities.

"Mama, maybe Brett would like a tour of the house."

The distraction worked. Glass of iced tea in hand,

Brett followed her mother through the wooden double doors of the entrance.

Rafaela eased back into her seat and, for the first time all afternoon, relaxed. Her injury must have been taking its toll, because when she next opened her eyes, the two were returning.

"If you're a fan of Pueblo style architecture, you would love Troy's home." The smile Rafaela found so charming slipped easily over Brett's lips.

"It sounds beautiful. I'd love to see it," her mother replied.

"The place is a work of art." His mischievous grin made Rafaela smile in spite of herself. "Maybe we can arrange a visit. I do know the owner, after all."

Laughing, her mother sat at the table beside Rafaela as Brett continued.

"Speaking of my friend, I noticed a stunning wood sculpture in the studio." Brett directed his statement to Rafaela as he sat and stretched out his long legs. "Are you familiar with the work of Troy Madrigal?"

"Of course." Everyone knew Madrigal's work. He was one of the leading artists in his field, but he hadn't produced a new work in almost five years.

"He and his wife Eliza are collaborating on some pieces, incorporating her glass into his wood work. They started after I left Sedona, so I haven't actually seen any of them, but from what Troy says, they're turning out well."

"That sounds…intriguing." *Understatement of the year.*

Madrigal's first major work after years dedicated to building his home and the Fallon School of Art. Had the time off inspired him or set him back?

Rafaela would give her eyeteeth for a peek at the

work, but she stomped on her excitement. "Is it something close to what Albert Wolkowski's doing?" An established wood sculptor, Wolkowski had been experimenting with stained glass in wood framed scenes.

"Great minds think alike." Brett placed his empty glass on the table. "That's exactly what I asked Troy. He says it's something totally different with a very Southwest feel."

Only Rafaela's sprained ankle kept her from jumping up and clapping her hands. It was high time something new and innovative burst on the scene to bring attention back to art in the Southwest. But she absolutely refused to impose on her newfound friendship and ask the questions she was dying to ask.

Her mother, however, had no such guilt-fed hindrances. "That sounds like a perfect fit for our gallery."

"Mother!"

"Well, it's true. You know you were thinking the same thing, Rafaela."

"*I* was just thinking how exciting the work sounded. I hadn't jumped that far ahead."

"Well, I did." Brett's low-timbre voice sent shivers over her again. "The minute I saw the horse in your gallery, I wondered about Troy's new work. Eliza's agent is anxious to handle the pieces, but he and Troy don't always agree. Troy feels it's time for a change. New work. New representation."

A part of Rafaela wanted to jump and shout again. But another, smaller part of her sank. Was that the reason for Brett's interest? He thought her gallery would be the perfect fit for his friend?

That reasoning sounded more likely than the

remote possibility that Brett Fraser, protégé of Daniel Fallon and boy wonder of the art world—until just recently—could possibly be interested in Rafaela.

The thought put things in perspective. Changed the whole situation and wiped away all the tension, irritability, and concern Rafaela had been experiencing since her mother first told her Brett was coming to dinner.

Of course his attention was rooted in business; the thing Rafaela did best. Now she could relax.

Brett mentioned several new artists, and Rafaela jumped into the conversation with enthusiasm now that she understood her guest. He had insights into her field and knowledge he seemed only too happy to share. Rafaela could have talked longer, but eventually her mother pointed to the distant sunset, just beginning to darken the bright sky with mauve.

"Perhaps we should eat. I'll go fetch Sofia. Then I'll bring our dinner out here."

"I can go after Sofia if you'd like to take care of the food," Brett offered.

Rafaela began to shake her head, but her mother spoke up.

"That would be wonderful. Thank you, Brett. If you go around this corner, you'll find her near the back fence."

Rafaela clamped her lips shut and waited until Brett had gone. "Mama, what are you thinking? You know how strangers and change upset Sofia."

"There's nothing Sofia likes better than painting. I don't think she'll mind that Brett's a stranger, especially since he knows so much about art."

Rafaela caught her breath. "That's why you did this, isn't it? You invited him out here so he would see

Sofia's paintings. You want him to use his influence to get her into the art school even after we decided it wasn't right for her."

Her mother rose slowly from the table, shaking her head all the while. "*You* decided the school wouldn't be good for her. I'm not so sure I agree. If Brett makes any offers to help, I won't rudely ignore them, as you have. But that's not the reason I invited him here. I have two daughters, and I'm concerned for *both* their welfares, not just the one." With that, she turned away and headed for the kitchen.

4

Brett rounded the corner of the house and came to a dead standstill. One corner of the large adobe fence was crumbling, falling down in dusty disrepair. The sun, centered in the "V" of the crumbling wall, began its descent, falling behind the distant hills. Three quarters gone, the golden orb radiated pale waves. Behind it, a mauve sky, darkened to gray. Dark green piñon pine trees dotted the red soil and flowed over the hill. The break in the adobe framed the distant scene perfectly—and just inside, not far from the broken portion, Sofia sat in front of an easel.

With her baggy sweater and spiked dark hair, she stood out against the sand-colored fence, her slender arm outstretched as she applied strokes to a canvas. If the painting was half as lovely as the scene in front of him, it would be brilliant.

For some reason Brett couldn't explain, he pulled out his camera and snapped a picture. The photo captured the strong beauty of the sunset and the fragility of the young girl. Stunning.

Brett hadn't missed the telltale signs of Sofia's illness. His closest friend, Lara Fallon, had nearly died in a devastating car accident. He'd spent years helping with her rehabilitation and accompanying her to specialized clinics, where he'd witnessed far too many young girls suffering from anorexia. He recognized those signs in Sofia de Silva.

He didn't know what caused it, or why she suffered so miserably, but one thing was certain—young Sofia had an eye for beauty.

Softening his steps, he moved forward.

Sofia must have heard him because she stopped painting. But she didn't turn around, just sat there with her back to him, frozen in time.

Brett studied the canvas without interruption and what he saw stunned him.

Sofia had softened the edges of the adobe wall and added a giant crack in the fence, which made the contrast with the beautiful sunset even more startling. Her efforts made it seem as if the sunset—no, nature itself—had burst through the wall and spilled through the man-made barrier to reclaim what it had lost. The girl had rendered an amazing interpretation. Lucia was right. Sofia was extremely talented.

All through his examination, Sofia stayed still, unmoving, as if waiting. Had she even breathed? Should he tell her work was amazing? Would she turn away from him, embarrassed, or appreciate the gesture? Truth was always the best choice, even when difficult.

He drew a slow, deep breath. "You realize it's brilliant, don't you?"

Sofia gave him a quick glance, and a smile flitted over her lips—but so briefly he almost missed it.

She turned her back to him again, but that small flash of a smile told him she was pleased. "My father would have called it fanciful."

"I call it evocative. It makes me think."

"My father was a great painter. What do you know about art?"

Her sharp words caught Brett off guard. Good to

know little Sofia possessed a bit of spark—like her older sister. The thought made him smile. "I know quite a lot, actually. But even if I were a nobody just looking at your painting, I would find it strikingly beautiful."

She gave a little shake of her head. "It's the rancho that's beautiful. I love it."

"I can see why."

Something in his tone must have conveyed his sincerity because she turned and met his gaze for the first time. "You said you know a lot about art. How?"

Brett smiled. "Look my name up online. You'll see all about me. In the meantime, your mother sent me to fetch you. Dinner is ready."

She made a small, displeased face. "I'm not very hungry and the light will be gone soon."

"Well, I'm starving and I have a feeling your mother won't let me start without you. Besides, the light will be here tomorrow night and the night after that."

"Fine." She huffed a little as she grabbed the painting and easel and strode back to the house. Brett had to do a hop-skip to catch up as she stopped at a shed and placed the easel inside. He caught a glimpse of canvases covered with brilliant sunsets, blooming cacti, and penciled hands in various unfinished forms before she shut the door with a pointed click and then marched toward the house.

Obviously he'd overstepped his bounds by forcing her to attend the dinner party. He hoped she wouldn't hold it against him and not eat the food her mother had prepared. Shaking his head, he hurried to catch up to the very opinionated Miss de Silva.

As soon as he came around the corner, distinctive

smells wafted toward him. His stomach reminded him with a very loud growl that it had been a long time since his last meal.

Sofia grinned and turned back to him. "You weren't lying. You are hungry."

"Hey, I never lie." *Sometimes I don't tell the entire truth but...*he didn't know where that wayward thought had come from. Probably his most recent history. But he wouldn't let the events in Sedona spoil this lovely evening, the great company, and the grand food.

Lucia had gone all out. Pico de Gallo salsa made from scratch and not too hot for his untutored mouth. Fresh flour tortillas, browned with a light touch. Pork carnitas sautéed with onions, bell peppers, and mouthwatering seasonings. Traditional rice and beans flavored with homemade goodness. Fresh crema for topping and sliced avocados for added flair.

Brett ate too much but couldn't seem to stop. Finally he pushed away from the table, even as Lucia offered him a bowl of flan. He peered at the dish. "I'm not even sure what it is but I know it will be spectacular. I just can't eat another bite."

"Flan is a custard with a caramel-flavored topping. I will send some home with you."

Brett patted his stomach. "Thank you. I'll enjoy trying it. But I see now why Rafaela runs every morning."

Lucia laughed. "I love to cook. It's been a while since I've had much time for it. I appreciate the opportunity. If you are planning to stay in Santa Fe, I would love to cook for you again."

"As a matter of fact..." Brett paused as all three women at the table turned to face him with different expressions.

Lucia seemed hopeful.

Curiosity painted Sofia's thin face.

Rafaela's expression bespoke displeasure. She was definitely displeased.

Ignoring her reaction, Brett focused on Lucia. "Actually, I find Santa Fe intriguing. I'm determined to explore every corner."

Lucia smiled.

Sofia cocked her head.

And Rafaela frowned.

Yes, he was most definitely staying to explore the interesting features Santa Fe had to offer, especially the most baffling Rafaela de Silva and her mixed signals.

~*~

A scream pierced the silent night.

Rafaela lunged upwards from her bed and pain shot from her ankle up her calf. Crying out, she doubled over before another scream rent the air.

Sofia. Ignoring the pain, Rafaela clutched her crutches and hobbled down the hallway to her sister's room.

Her mother was already there, arms circling a crumpled Sofia.

"Another nightmare?"

Her mother nodded, her expression sad and strained.

"Not another one," Sofia sobbed. "The same nightmare, over and over again. I'm falling and falling and it never ends. Then I see Papa below me, with his arms wide, waiting to catch me. But when I fall into his arms, he's decayed, half-eaten by worms. I can't bear to see him like that, Mama. Make it stop! Make the dream stop!"

"Oh, *mija*, you know I would if I could. But the doctor says only you can stop the dream…you know that. You must try, *mi amor*. Try not to be so afraid."

"I do try, Mama. Then the lights and the sounds come. I try and try to go back to sleep, but I can't, and if I do…then the nightmare comes again."

"The lights and sounds…" Mama's words trailed off, sounding disheartened. For months now, Sofia claimed sounds and lights flashed in her room, waking her. She described the sounds as dark rumblings, like a monster coming out of the depths of the ground and the lights as flashes out of the sky.

Rafaela and her mother had investigated, searching the house, the grounds and the area surrounding the house, to no avail. They'd even taken turns sleeping with Sofia. But each time, nothing had happened. No strange events occurred and Sofia slept soundly through the night.

Her sister's doctor suggested the incidents were yet another piece of Sofia's imagination, a way to keep her mother and sister close, to create the security she seemed to have lost after the death of her beloved father.

Neither Rafaela nor her mother wanted to believe the doctor's suggestion.

But the months went on and Sofia's claims continued…even though no one else ever witnessed the strange events.

Rafaela hated to admit it, but her sister was sinking deeper and deeper into the grip of her illness.

"Please, mija, try to forget the dream and go back to sleep." Her mother's coaxing fell on deaf ears.

"No. I want to paint. I need to paint."

Rafaela sighed and turned back to her room. All her mother's persuasive efforts would do no good.

Sofia would have her way. She'd fret and worry until their mother let her up. Then she'd turn on the lights and paint with a manic obsession, not ceasing for hours, or sometime days, rarely stopping to drink and never eating until she was too weak to hold the brush.

Rafaela eased back onto her bed, her foot throbbing.

Sofia's doctor had recommended a specialist in Phoenix. Maybe now was the time…before it was too late.

Somehow, someway, Rafaela had to find the money. Perhaps she should accept Tío Aaron's offer. As much as Rafaela hated to even consider it, the rancho was not more important to her than her sister's life—and Sofia's health was definitely deteriorating.

It wasn't as if they'd have to leave. Tío knew how much they loved this place. Rancho de Silva was the only home they'd ever known…all that was left to them of their father and their rich heritage. Tío had suggested that Rafaela allow him to buy the land simply because through him, they could stay rent-free in the house their great-grandfather had built. If they sold to anyone else, they would be forced to move. The amount Tío would pay for the land would give them the security they needed.

As much as the idea of living with no worries about money appealed to Rafaela, she'd never been able to relinquish hold of the land that had belonged to her family for generations. Rafaela wasn't even sure she could stay in Santa Fe if she sold the property. But none of that was as important as Sofia's health. If selling to Tío meant Rafaela could send her mother and little sister to Phoenix, then selling is what she would do.

A light flipped on in the hall and crawled along the space beneath Rafaela's door.

Her mother's quiet tones and Sofia's more strident response drifted in along with the light.

So...another marathon painting session had begun.

Rafaela turned on her side, away from the door, debating whether to take a pain pill. If only her mother had listened. Having Brett Fraser as a dinner guest had obviously upset her sister. He was the reason for this outburst. Although, Sofia had seemed very comfortable with their witty visitor after they'd returned to the house together.

What exactly had they discussed on their walk? Sofia had seemed more attentive and actually listened to the dinner conversation. Usually, she tuned them out, rarely taking part in anything Rafaela and her mother discussed. The only thing Sofia cared about was painting.

Had Brett managed to tap into her sister's secret life? Did she allow him to see her work?

Rafaela hadn't seen any of Sofia's paintings in almost six months.

Her sister had become so mysterious, even their mother wasn't allowed to view what Sofia painted.

If Brett had seen her paintings, how did he manage it? How did he charm her fragile, but willful sister?

What a ridiculous question.

Brett Fraser possessed more than his fair share of charm. Apparently his brand of magnetism worked on young girls as well as older women and every age in between. He'd managed to sway all the de Silva women...herself included.

But that was about to end. As much as she had appreciated his help—and maybe the man himself—Brett would not gain any more access to her life. She could not allow him to upset her sister again.

~*~

Brett meant what he'd told the de Silva women. The quaint, Pueblo style town with its own brand of culture intrigued him. He woke the next morning with the intention of exploring Santa Fe and its unique sights.

The Loretto Chapel, not far from his hotel, had a rich history. Built in the 1800s, it included a miraculous set of wooden stairs with three hundred sixty degree turns and no apparent means of support. The chapel also boasted a beautiful stained-glass window, made in Paris. The window came across the Atlantic in a sailing ship, then to Saint Louis in a paddle boat and across the Santa Fe Trail by covered wagon to its home in the chapel.

A museum tour of the Palace of the Governors led him through the historic adobe building built in the seventeenth century. As the seat of the government, the building chronicled the rich history of New Mexico and the Southwest.

Enticing smells pulled him toward a small corner restaurant where he sampled tamales. The savory dish was good but not as good as the home-cooked meal Lucia de Silva had served him last night.

Wary of taxing the de Silva hospitality, he tried to

stay away. But an examination of the various shops and galleries around the plaza inevitably led him to a comparison. The de Silva shop stood apart. Rafaela definitely had a flair for display and appeal. Perhaps it was her use of color, distinct and understated, so like the woman herself.

Brett had the feeling deep passion and fire lay banked beneath her reserved surface. He could sense it in her style and see it in the bright splashes of color in her dress and shop. Why did she keep it hidden? What emotion was she trying so desperately to suppress?

He stood in front of the de Silva shop, looking through the big plate-glass window, examining the art Rafaela had chosen and how it stood out against the backdrop of muted colors.

Lucia came from the back of the shop, carrying a painting. She waved, gesturing him to come inside. "I was hoping you'd stop by today." She propped the painting against a desk tucked into a corner. "I wanted to thank you for staying for dinner last night."

"Thank me? I should be thanking you. That's the first home-cooked meal I've had in…well, let's just say a long time."

Lucia ducked her head and gave a graceful shake. "You were very kind to Sofia and I think…she enjoyed your company."

Brett smiled. "I enjoyed hers. She has spunk, like her sister, whom I think we can both agree did not enjoy my company so much."

"That's why I hoped to see you. Please, don't make the mistake of misreading Rafaela. She likes you, but she worries too much, I think."

"About me?"

She gave another graceful shake. "About Sofia,

41

me, everything. Rafaela feels responsible for us all. You see, Sofia had…an episode last night, and I fear Rafaela may use the incident to push you away. I don't want you to think you are at fault when it's really all about us."

"I don't understand. Why would Rafaela blame me and why would she want to push me away?"

She fingered the painting. "It's a long, sad story. I don't want to bore you."

A wry grin slipped out. "Trust me. Nothing you could say about Rafaela will bore me. What kind of an episode did Sofia have?"

The older woman heaved a great sigh. "She woke screaming in the middle of the night. About a year ago, she started hearing sounds and lights that no one else sees. Ever since then she's had difficulty sleeping, which only adds to her strain and health issues."

"And Rafaela thinks *I* am to blame?"

"She hasn't said so yet, but I'm sure she will. You see, I surprised both of my girls with your invitation to dinner. Rafaela is convinced the best way to help her sister is to keep her environment controlled, no changes, no issues to confront. She believes if Sofia has nothing to fear, she will relinquish the tight control she tries to maintain over every aspect of her life, especially her eating."

"You don't agree?"

She fingered the painting again. "I don't know for sure. Sometimes I think the best thing for Sofia is to help her conquer her fears, not to shelter her from them. At other times, I think it's my own desire to break free that drives me."

Her words gave him pause. "What chains do you wish to break?"

Lifting the painting, she held it in front of her and studied it. "Chains of love, Brett," she said, not lifting her gaze. "Chains that bind us even after death."

5

Brett's reaction must have shown because she laughed. "You shouldn't be surprised. Surely you've seen it. My husband was larger than life. Passionate. Talented. Creative. He consumed the world and everything around him. Naturally we were swallowed up by his strong personality. He was so charismatic and oh, how he loved us."

She shook her head and turned her gaze back to Brett. "He was our driving force. When he was gone, we didn't know how to go on. It took us a long time to even try. Then Rafaela took charge, tried to make things as they had been before. Subconsciously, Sofia bound up our wounds by focusing our energies on her health and I...I lost myself in blame. I realized too late that we'd placed our trust in Rafael's human hands when all along it should have been in the Lord's." Drawing a deep breath, she straightened. "I finally put away the guilt. Now I try to focus on rebuilding our lives. I've prayed and prayed for direction to lead my girls."

She fixed her dark gaze on Brett, and a half-panicked sensation sank to the pit of his stomach. Was she looking to him for direction? Did she see him as some kind of knight in shining armor?

If he could, he would help this kind woman who had touched him with her tender ways. But Brett knew only too well that trying to be the hero would lead to failure. Trying to walk that path had destroyed his life and future in Sedona. He wasn't about to make the same mistake again. "Lucia…"

Holding up a hand, she smiled a lovely, knowing smile that warmed his heart. "Please, don't think I'm trying to replace one strong man in our lives with another. I've learned my lesson, and I have no such expectations, Brett. My faith is firmly entrenched in God."

A part of him sighed with relief. Another flinched with regret. He wanted to be a hero. To do right in God's eyes. But somehow, he never measured up. He seemed to forever miss the important clues and markers. His faith simply wasn't where it needed to be.

"But I do take your arrival in our lives as a sign, Brett. Why else would Sofia respond so favorably to you? She doesn't even speak to her Tío Aaron, and he's been a part of her life since the day she was born. You are not our savior, Brett, but your friendship is a gift from God. Will you be our friend?"

That was easy. In fact, there was nothing Brett would like better than befriending the de Silvas. His accidental meeting with Rafaela almost seemed to be part of a plan. He certainly hoped so. The thought made him grin. "Only if you promise to be my friend, too. I could use one of those."

"Deal." She attempted to hold out her hand for a shake, but the large painting she'd been clutching got in her way.

Brett laughed. "Here, let me take that. Can I hang it somewhere for you?"

"No, it's not for display. I was feeling a bit melancholy and pulled out my husband's favorite piece. He painted his father, Rafaela's grandfather, at home in front of his collection."

The older man had a shock of white hair and a thick mustache. The rich colors and perfection of his body shape were the first things that caught Brett's eye. Rafael de Silva was a master of painting the human form. One could almost see the pride in the old man's features as he fingered the piece of pottery on the mantel.

And that's where Brett's gaze riveted. A chill washed over his entire body and sent ripples down his spine.

The pottery on the mantel was an exquisite, distinctive piece of ancient Chaco pottery. Brett had seen it before—in the display case of his good friend Troy Madrigal.

Illegally obtained, black market Chaco pottery was the cause of Brett's troubles in Sedona. The reason for his downfall.

Now, the piece that triggered suspicion and the attention of Homeland Security had appeared in a painting belonging to the de Silvas?

Brett's heavenly connection with the women became more than wishful thinking. Now it appeared to be ordained. Had God brought him to Santa Fe so he could redeem himself?

~*~

Rafaela situated herself in the open courtyard to catch the late afternoon sun. Juggling the crutches, she'd still managed to angle the chaise longue so she could see Sofia.

In a room off the courtyard, her sister had been painting with manic obsession since awakening early in the morning. Twice, Rafaela had tried to get Sofia to stop and eat, at the very least to drink something.

But her sister had ignored her, almost as if she were punishing Rafaela for not believing her about the night sounds.

Rafaela tried. She wanted to believe Sofia. But her sister didn't make it easy. After months of bizarre behavior and passive-aggressive temper tantrums like today, Rafaela found it hard to have faith in Sofia. In fact, it was hard even to have hope. Would they ever find their way out of this maze of depression and helplessness? She leaned her head back. Perhaps it was the pain talking, making her feel more like a victim. She was certainly more tired. She closed her eyes...just for a moment.

Rafaela jerked awake. *I must have dozed off. What was that sound?* Her gaze flew to her sister.

Sofia was lying on the ground, her uncoiled palm open and a tilted paintbrush over her fingertips.

Oh, no. No, no. I knew it. Just knew it. Why didn't she listen to me?

Clutching her crutches, Rafaela hobbled across the floor, punching her mother's cellphone number as she made step-by-step progress. She still hadn't reached her sister's prone body when her mother's soothing voice echoed over the line. "Mom, it's Sofia. She's collapsed."

Not waiting for a response, she tucked the phone back into the bag attached to her crutches then knelt beside her sister. Crutches clattered against the tiles as they fell, ignored. Rafaela lifted Sofia's head onto her lap.

Her sister's lips were pale and cracked from lack of fluids. Sofia's long, dark eyelashes rested against pale cheeks, just as they had when she was little. Her thin, almost emaciated, cheeks made her look younger. Like a small child.

Rafaela's heart nearly burst with sorrow. Tears filled her eyes and traced a hot path down her cheeks. "Sofia, please. Please wake up."

Her sister's eyes fluttered open.

"Oh, thank you, Lord." Rafaela's words came out with a sob and she hugged Sofia's frail form close.

"What happened?"

"You fainted again."

Sofia tried to rise but Rafaela pushed her back down onto her lap. "No, just rest a moment. You're weak. You might fall again."

Sofia touched the wet path tears had made on Rafaela's cheek. "I'm sorry. I didn't mean to frighten you."

The sincerity in her tone gave Rafaela pause. "Hush." She pushed the spiky, dark hair off Sofia's head. "I know you didn't mean to do it, but you should have listened to me. You are still weak from your last episode. You needed to rest."

Sofia's eyes drooped closed. "I *am* thirsty."

Rafaela laughed. "Well, by the time I manage to get up, Mama will probably be here."

"You called Mama?" Her little sister's eyes flew wide.

"Of course I did. I can't very well lift you or help you, can I?" She tried to soften the reality of the situation. She knew how much Sofia hated hospitals and doctors. Telling her sister she was probably headed there might result in another rebellious teenage response, and Rafaela simply wasn't ready to deal with that.

Rafaela eased Sofia's head off her lap and reached for the nearest crutch.

Ignoring the warning to stay still, Sofia reached for the other. The effort cost her, and when she'd handed the crutch to Rafaela, she leaned back with her eyes closed, spent by that simple effort.

Determined to keep her thoughts off her own body's weakness, Rafaela pulled the crutches beneath her and rose quickly to her feet, creating another jolt of pain. Gritting her teeth, she rose to her full height. "What flavor would you like?" They kept a wide variety of sport drinks in the fridge in hopes of tempting Sofia. "I know the blue kind is your favorite."

Her sister's long pause caused Rafaela a moment of panic. Had Sofia changed her mind? Was she going to be obstinate about taking the drink? Rafaela glanced back over her shoulder and almost tripped over one of her crutches. Another jolt of pain. She froze. Drew a deep breath and calmed her jumping senses.

"Yes, the blue. Bring two, OK?"

Rafaela sighed with relief and then carefully moved forward. Dropping the drinks in her bag, she returned to her sister and helped her rise. She opened the tight lid of the drink and almost spilled it, juggling it with her arms wrapped around Sofia.

Sofia chuckled. "Look at us. We are a pair, sitting here on the floor."

Rafaela smiled. "Yes, we are a pair. And don't you forget it." She gave a meaningful squeeze to Sofia's shoulder.

Sofia ducked her head and nodded. Only a slight nod, but it reassured Rafaela.

The crunch of wheels in the driveway announced the arrival of their mother. She hurried through the propped-open gate with Brett Fraser close behind.

Rafaela's breath caught. What was her mother thinking? The last thing Sofia needed was another stranger in her environment. She would already resist a trip to the emergency room. Brett's presence would make the girl even more withdrawn. Rafaela braced herself, waiting for the inevitable reaction.

Her mother shot Rafaela a glance before she dropped to the ground beside them. "That old truck broke down again. I couldn't get it started." With that quick explanation, her mother turned her attention to her sister. "Sofia, my love, what have you done?"

"I'm sorry, Mama. Don't be mad."

Their mother shook her head. "Sofia, Sofia, when am I ever mad?"

Never. You're never mad. You never lose patience with her, even when I'm ready to strangle her. Maybe if once, just once you'd let her know…

"But"—her mother's voice interrupted Rafaela's silent rant. A thread of steel Rafaela had never heard before firmed her mother's words—"You will have to go to the hospital."

"No, Mama. Really, I'm fine. I just overdid it."

"There will be no argument, Sofia. You're going to be checked out. You are probably dehydrated and too weak. I'll not risk more permanent damage. We *will* go. I've already called Tío Aaron. He's on his way."

Brett stepped closer. "In the meantime, how about if we get you two off the floor?"

Without pause, he scooped Sofia's frail body into his arms. To Rafaela's amazement her sister didn't protest. To her greater surprise, Sofia murmured, "Can't *you* take me to the hospital in your car?"

The sweet, tender smile Brett gave Sofia warmed

Rafaela's heart in a way she'd never dreamed possible.

"If I could, little one, we'd already be on our way. But I only have two seats in that car of mine. There's not room for you, your mother and me. So Tío Aaron is on his way."

He gently settled Sofia on the chaise where Rafaela had dozed. Hadn't that been ages ago? Then he returned for Rafaela.

"Oh, no! I can walk. I'm too heavy."

Brett's frown told her just how silly she sounded. His arms were around her so quickly that she didn't have time to protest. He scooped her close, and a light aftershave tickled her nose. Strong arms clasped around her waist and thighs and a rock-hard chest pressed against her cheek.

With one lunge, he lifted to his full height. Rafaela soared upwards and she gasped, not sure if it was the sudden movement or the sensation of the slender, wiry strength of his body.

He smelled wonderful. The rough texture of his shirt rasped against her cheek, but she didn't even try to move away.

All too suddenly, it was over, and he eased her onto the chaise next to Sofia. For a moment, his scent lingered, and she wished his arms were still around her. When she realized where her thoughts had gone, embarrassment washed through her. She dared not meet his gaze for fear he'd know what prompted her red cheeks. Flustered, she mumbled her thanks then turned to her sister and mother, seated on the chaise beside her.

"Rafaela, you look flushed. Are you in pain again?"

Thank you, Mother, for noticing.

Carefully keeping her gaze averted from Brett, she nodded. "Yes, I am a little."

Her mother handed her the second sport drink. "Here, drink this. I'll fetch another for Sofia."

"Let me get it." Brett guided her mother to a seat and headed for the kitchen.

With his back toward her, Rafaela felt safe enough to watch him as he walked away. Why hadn't she noticed his loose-limbed walk before? He seemed so comfortable in his own skin, so sure of himself. Who would have known there was so much strength behind that lithe body? Still staring at the doorway, she quickly looked away when he returned.

Fortunately, another car pulled into the driveway. Tío Aaron, of course. Thankful for the distraction, Rafaela focused on the entrance. Tío came through, his broad shoulders barely clearing the double doors of the gate.

Was it her imagination or did he hesitate when he saw Brett? Tío's gaze shot to Mama and Sofia. He crossed the courtyard with huge strides and was beside them in an instant.

Did Sofia shy away when he came close? Did his hand stay longer on Mama's shoulder than normal?

Ridiculous. Shock...or the drugs prescribed for Rafaela's pain were responsible for her heightened senses. Shock *and* drugs. Surely they were causing her to see things that weren't there and feel things she shouldn't. Certainly, she was out of control. The best thing would be for Tío Aaron to take Mama and Sofia to the hospital and for Brett to return to his hotel.

Soon. Before Rafaela said or did something stupid.

Tío Aaron picked up Sofia and turned to Brett. "Thanks once again for your help, Mr. Fraser. I'll be sure to let you know about Sofia's progress."

A wry smile slipped over Brett's lips. "Thanks for your consideration but that won't be necessary. I'm staying with Rafaela until we get a diagnosis."

Oh, no. I'm in serious, serious trouble.

6

Lucia and Aaron loaded a very weak Sofia into Aaron's car. The quiet rumble of the auto echoed over the valley until the car climbed the hill. When the sound finally faded, silence settled over Brett and Rafaela like a heavy blanket.

Rafaela's features twisted into a combination of discomfort and annoyance.

Did his presence really make her that uncomfortable? Hiding his smile, he placed his hands on his hips. "Have you eaten?"

Her lips parted and her eyes widened. "You don't have to do this, you know. I'm quite capable of managing on my own."

"And you are quite incapable of accepting a helping hand when it's offered."

"I can accept help…when I know the reason behind the offer. For the life of me, I can't understand why you are making yourself so available to us."

Brett's gaze slipped over her thick, dark hair resting over one shoulder and then touched on her brown eyes, so deep and fathomless, and lips that were almost red. How could she not know how incredibly beautiful she was? He shook his head and leveled his gaze on her. "Are my reasons really a mystery to you, Rafaela? Do you not know why I'm here?"

For some reason, she could no longer meet his gaze. She looked away. "I-I'm not free, Brett. I think that should be painfully obvious. I don't have time for a relationship. My mother and sister need me."

"Having a relationship won't exclude them, Rafaela. Besides, your mother and your sister seem to enjoy my company. In fact, if you asked me, I'd say your sister doesn't like your Tío Aaron."

Her gaze jerked up. "You noticed that too? I thought it was my imagination."

Brett shook his head. "She definitely shied away from him when he bent to pick her up."

"I know she's not fond of him. But—"

"Her reaction was more than just a lack of fondness. She seemed afraid."

"I don't understand. They've never argued or had a falling out that I'm aware. I know she resents his authority. Since our father's death, he's helped us so much with finances, taxes, everything. Sofia was too young to understand and thought he was trying to take our father's place."

"I think maybe she understood more than you realize."

She stared at him and a variety of different emotions played over her features. Surprise. Sadness. Understanding.

"Are you so sure Aaron wouldn't like to take your father's place?"

She heaved a sigh. "No. I'm not sure." She shifted uncomfortably. "I'm not sure about anything right now. My world seems to be turning topsy-turvy."

"Is that such a bad thing?" He couldn't help the smile that slid over his lips.

Her posture stiffened. "They just took my sister to urgent care. What do you think?"

"Sofia's illness needs treatment, but it's not related

to my being here. She seems perfectly fine with my presence. You're the only one who seems to have an issue. Am I such a problem?"

"Yes." The little laugh that burst from her held more sarcasm than amusement. "You scare me to death. You're handsome and have rich and famous friends. You drive around in a car that would pay the back taxes on my home and all my bills. You don't even have to work! You march into our lives like a bright, shining star and light up everything around us. But I don't know why you are here or how long you will stay. I especially don't know how we'll handle the dark when you leave again. Yes, Brett Fraser. You are a *serious* problem for me."

"So...you think I'm handsome?" A silly grin slipped out. He couldn't stop it. He didn't want to. It made him crazy-happy that she thought him handsome. If he had his head on straight, he'd worry that this little sign of affection gave him so much pleasure. And that it was the *only* sign he'd received from Ms. Rafaela de Silva. He should be scared witless. Instead, he felt that silly grin coming on again.

"Yes, I think you're handsome. Maybe too handsome for your own good. Your charm has my mother and even my sister wrapped around your finger."

He thought of his recent troubles in Sedona and shook his head. "I promise you, not so many people find me charming. Perhaps your mom and sister just recognize a genuine desire for friendship. Can't we just be friends?"

She laughed. "I guess so. Especially since that's the death knell for a romance—when a partner asks to be 'just friends.'"

Brett had walked right into that one and decided not to attempt a smart reply. He had no idea where this relationship was going, but he had no intention of this being the death knell. Rafaela lit sparks inside him. For the last six months he'd felt dead. He needed sparks, and he wasn't walking away unless ordered.

He needed Rafaela, and her family needed support. A match made in heaven, right? And since he'd seen that piece of pottery in the painting at the gallery, he was certain the Divine hand was in action. Nothing short of a command to leave would keep him from moving forward with this relationship now. "Since that's settled, let's get back to my original question. Have you eaten today?"

She ducked her head. "No. I haven't had much appetite, and, well, I've been preoccupied with Sofia."

"That's what I thought." Not waiting for a response, he scooped her off the chaise and marched to the kitchen. A soft, flowery scent drifted up to him. What was it? Jasmine? Camellia? He couldn't place it.

Several high stools butted up to a tiled breakfast bar. He paused by one stool. "If you will pull that out for me."

Rafaela tugged the chair out and he eased her onto the seat. Then he pulled out another and gently lifted her legs into place. "Do you need a pillow?"

She shook her head.

Brett didn't miss the dull red beneath the lovely olive tone of her cheeks. Apparently, she wasn't as unaffected by his "charm" as she claimed. Smiling to himself, he opened the refrigerator. "Just as I thought, leftover enchiladas. We'll have a feast. Did I tell you how much I enjoyed your mother's cooking?"

"Quite a number of times."

"Oh. Well, a home-cooked meal after months of fast-food is a real treat."

As he placed a healthy portion of microwave-warmed enchilada onto a plate for Rafaela, he guided her away from sensitive topics. "Tell me about that distinctive wood statue in your gallery."

Her gaze flashed with surprise. "You noticed it?"

"Absolutely stunning. And highlighting it right in the center of the gallery was a brilliant move on your part."

"I'm so glad you noticed." Even her tone seemed to warm. "The artist is Emilio Gonzales. He lives at one of the Pueblos. We've been friends since we were children, and I've always loved his work, but he has only recently come into his own as an artist."

"I can see why. It's a standout piece. I thought most Pueblos were closed to outsiders. If Emilio lives there, how is it that you and he have been friends since you were children?"

"Only the old Taos Pueblo is closed to most outsiders. But my family has always had close ties with all nineteen of the Pueblo tribes. As a young boy, my grandfather roamed the land on horseback with two other childhood friends. One of them grew up to become a tribe elder. My grandfather was one of the first men to display Native American artwork in his gallery."

"I saw your father's painting of your grandfather today. He was holding an incredible piece of Chaco pottery." Just like that their conversation drifted into the territory Brett needed to explore.

"Yes. In his late teens, my grandfather discovered a mound on our property. Just a mound in the ground along a wash, but buried beneath were some incredible ancient artifacts—the remains of a woven sandal, and a fantastic feather cape. Of course, in those days, they didn't know about much excavation. Still, my grandfather was very careful with the digging. His friends helped him. By the time they finished, he had quite a collection of artifacts and clay pot remnants. He donated the sandal and the cape to the University of New Mexico for study, and kept most of the Chaco pottery. But that pitcher was his prize possession. I was devastated when I had to sell it."

"You sold it?" Brett tried to keep the surprise out of his voice. These were the answers he needed but that didn't stop the wave of guilt that swept over him. Friends didn't secretly pump friends for information. He felt like a hypocrite after having just asked for her trust and friendship...but not guilty enough to stop from asking the burning question in his mind.

"Who *did* you sell it to? A private collector?"

"I don't know who it went to. I couldn't handle it myself so I asked Tío Aaron to do it for me. I thought that would be better."

Tío Aaron again. The man kept popping up like a bad smell. Had he sold the piece directly to Louis Ferone? Or to a dealer who then sold it to Brett's good friend Troy Madrigal?

Either way, the piece had ended up in Troy's collection and caused him to be investigated by Homeland Security. The whole Fallon School of Art, including Brett as its director, had come under scrutiny by the Immigration and Customs Enforcement, a branch of Homeland Security.

I.C.E. was tracking the path of illegally obtained Chaco pottery sold on the black market. They suspected the Fallon School of Art had received the stolen artifacts, and then shipped them to international buyers. An old enemy of Daniel Fallon's had done a very good job of implicating the school.

Of course, the devious plot was uncovered. Arrests were made, but the source—the all-important site of the ancient Chaco artifacts—was never discovered.

Troy and the school were cleared, but Brett, as director of operations, never felt absolved. The whole debacle had occurred under his watch, and he'd missed it. From that point on, he'd considered himself unworthy to hold a position of trust in Daniel Fallon's company. He'd resigned and embarked on this self-imposed exile.

Now, it seemed the Lord had put him in a position to exonerate himself. By God's good grace, Brett had landed right at the source of the ancient artifacts. Even though the pitcher had been legally obtained, it had followed the same path as the illegal artifacts. If Brett could trace the path of the pitcher, perhaps he could discover the ancient site being systematically pillaged. Then maybe he could face Daniel Fallon again.

He was relieved to know the black-on-white Chaco pitcher ensconced in Troy's home had been obtained in a legal manner, and that the de Silvas were in no way implicated in illegal trafficking. At the turn of the century, laws had been enacted to prevent pothunters from robbing ancient artifacts from Native American or federally owned lands. However, if the site was on privately owned land, the owner had the right to excavate the site and sell any artifacts discovered.

Rafaela's grandfather had legally obtained all of his collection, and she was free to sell those pieces, provided they were accompanied with a Letter of Provenance, declaring the pieces had been discovered on privately owned land.

To the best of Brett's knowledge, however, Troy had not received such a document. Why hadn't Aaron Pomeroy included a letter with the sale? More importantly, did Brett dare question Rafaela and create suspicion when he'd just asked for her trust?

Rafaela pushed her empty plate away and leaned back against the back of the stool with closed eyes. She sagged, looking so weary.

Brett ached for her. His resolve hardened. Rafaela didn't need the additional stress or concern. He'd research Aaron Pomeroy himself. He didn't know how he would go about it, or even where he'd start. But for the time being, he'd keep Rafaela out of it.

"Come on. You look like you could use some rest." Not waiting for her response, he lifted her off the stool and headed toward the living room sofa. He heard the little sigh she released as he eased her onto the soft cushions and propped a pillow beneath her knee. He spread a blanket over her. She glanced across the courtyard and made a small sound.

"What is it?"

"Sofia's painting. If she comes home and sees it, she'll try to pick it right back up."

"Would you like me to move it?"

Rafaela raised her gaze to his. Those rich brown eyes made Brett feel as if he'd dived into a pool of warm, sweet chocolate. She could ask him to do just about anything and he'd obey right now. Fortunately, she only asked him to move the painting to the studio on the side of the house.

He left her with the television remote in her hands

and crossed the courtyard. Gathering a handful of the paints and brushes, he strode across the moonlit yard. Flagstones marked the path, and the studio door was unlocked. He stepped inside and paused. One whole side of the studio was floor-to-ceiling glass. A full moon spilled light into the small room, lighting everything with a silvery glow.

At the back of the studio was a small loft with a bed and a door that led to what appeared to be a bathroom. Beneath the loft, canvases filled oversized, vertical storage bins. On his right, a sink held an assortment of brushes in jars. Paints were stored in a nearby cabinet.

The studio was perfectly arranged and completely self-contained. Many artists would've given their right arm for a studio so perfectly appointed, yet Sofia chose to paint in a small, dark room in the main house where her sister and mother were forced to watch her self-destructive behavior.

Maybe that was the point.

Shaking his head, he found the light switch, flipped it on, and then headed back for the canvas and the easel. He glanced through the living room window as he passed. Just as he suspected, Rafaela was sound asleep. Certain now that he would not disturb her, he flipped on the light and studied the painting Sofia had been so determined to create.

A black night sky filled the painting. Stars dotted the sky, but lights flashed upwards, in a strange pattern. He realized Sofia was attempting to re-create headlights flashing in the night sky. The imagery was off; she hadn't quite captured the effect.

A large round hill filled the foreground. The lights came from behind it. Sofia's skill—not yet fully developed—was not up to re-creating the image, so the lights looked distorted and off, but Brett was certain he was looking at car headlights moving behind a dark hill. The whole scene looked familiar, as if he'd seen it some place.

Just as he was about to place the scene in his head, the low rumble of a car's engine reached his ears. He grabbed the painting and the easel, carried it out to the workshop, placed the easel at the back of the studio, and mounted the canvas in a corner where it wouldn't be seen at first glance. Then he flipped off the light and hurried to the courtyard gate just as the car stopped.

Lucia helped Sofia climb out of the front seat of Aaron's sedan.

Brett hurried forward.

When Sofia looked up, a ghost of a smile flitted over her lips.

"So they decided to let her come home?"

Lucia nodded. "She was only slightly dehydrated but in her weakened state, it was too much. They gave her an I.V. drip of fluids and sent her home with a stern warning."

Sofia set her slender little chin in a firm line.

Brett wasn't sure how much impact the "stern" warning would have. The girl had her mind set on something. Maybe he needed to be just as determined to find out what she wanted to accomplish. "You left Aaron in town?"

Lucia nodded. "He has an early flight. He'll be gone for over a week on a business trip, so he said we could use his car while he's gone. Honestly, that truck is giving us more trouble than it's worth lately. I wish we could afford something more dependable."

"Rafaela's asleep on the sofa. I left some dishes in

the kitchen. As soon as I clean those up, I'll be on my way."

Lucia looked back over her shoulder as she helped Sofia to her bedroom. "Thank you, Brett. I can't tell you how nice it's been to have your help."

Sofia stopped abruptly and turned back. "You will come back and visit us tomorrow, won't you? He can come to dinner again, can't he, Mama?"

"Of course. We would love to have him." Lucia's smile warmed Brett to the core and made him feel as if he'd done something wonderful when all he'd really done was offer a friendly hand.

"Will you come?" Sofia's fragile features were so open and vulnerable it tore at his heart.

"Are you kidding? I wouldn't miss more of your mother's home cooking."

Sofia gave a real smile, and Brett walked to the kitchen with a bounce in his step. The bright feeling lasted the whole time it took to wash up the dishes and say goodbye to Lucia. The smile even remained as he pulled away from the house. In fact, he was still feeling happy when he turned a corner and started the incline out of the valley. That's when he saw the hill and recognized it from Sofia's painting. Brett hit the brakes and came to skittering halt on the road.

Sofia had attempted to paint this very hill but with lights reflecting behind it. Why?

Obviously she'd passed this place a thousand times in her lifetime. Was it just a place or did it have meaning to her? Was this where she saw the mysterious lights?

He released the brake and eased forward. Brett angled his car to shine the lights along the side of the road. The white light illuminated sagebrush and piñon, but that was all. About to turn away, he caught a glimpse of something. Placing the car in park, he climbed out and hop-skipped down the steep, slippery embankment. Sure enough, behind a particularly tall piñon tree, two tracks became visible...a path that led into the desert. Stooping, Brett saw the squiggly tread of tires.

Was this the message Sofia was trying to deliver in her painting, to capture on canvas the sights that kept her awake? The nightmare sounds and lights that everyone claimed came from her vivid imagination?

Bret rose slowly. His sports car wasn't made for off-roading, but as soon as he could, he would follow this path and see where it led.

7

"Laurie, I appreciate the offer but we're doing just fine." Rafaela held her breath, hoping her comment would end the phone conversation.

"Are you sure, Rafe, you know how you hate to admit you might have a problem."

The high-pitched voice grated against nerves already strung tight. Her high school friend had no intention of letting Rafaela off the hook, or off the phone. What was her real objective? The woman had never been known for lending any kind of helping hand.

"Really, Laurie, we're doing just fine."

"Come on, Rafe, I know Jan is on vacation. You can't possibly handle the shop with your ankle."

Oh, how Rafaela hated the shortened, male version of her name Laurie had used since they were in junior high. Actually, it had only recently started to bother her—since she'd begun to suspect Laurie never really called to "catch up" but to pump her for information.

"I know you need the help. I've got a couple of free days since Jason is in Denver." Laurie's husband traveled a lot for his business. Too much. If he stayed home more often, maybe Laurie wouldn't be so desperate for company.

Rafaela tried one more time to put a stop to the offers. "That's kind of you, Laurie, but it really won't be necessary. My mom is taking care of the gallery for me."

"Your mom? How can she possibly be away from Sofia that long? This is way too much stress for you all."

Rafaela squirmed again, wishing she could just hang up. Laurie's statement was too close to the truth. "We'll manage."

"That's the point. You don't need to. Let me help. I'll pop on over there first thing tomorrow morning."

Something cold crawled its way through Rafaela's insides. If she'd had any doubts about Laurie's motives, they fled in the path of her friend's determination to get inside the gallery.

Fortunately, a car door opened and Brett walked into the courtyard.

Rafaela's pulse quickened. Normally she'd hate that little betrayal—the little sign that Brett meant more to her than just a casual friend. Those responses were not the kind she needed to have. But today he provided an escape from Laurie.

"Thanks for the offer, Laurie, but we really are managing just fine at the gallery. If we need help I'll give you a call. I have to run now. I have a visitor. Thanks again for the offer." She clicked off before Laurie could argue, and smiled as Brett situated himself on the lounge beside her.

"Nice. A friend offering to help?"

Rafaela laughed. "Not really."

Brett cocked his head. "That sounds like an interesting but long story. Let me check in with your mother. If she doesn't need any help with dinner, I'll be right back." He returned a few moments later with two glasses of something sparkling. "Your mother ordered me to sit and relax with these. Although I don't know why. She's the one who put in a full day at the gallery."

"She told me you took care of my truck and the repair shop. Thanks."

"Yep. I had it towed. Your mechanic, Joe, seems like a great guy. He was really upset that it broke down again. Said you just had it in."

"I did. I can't imagine what's wrong now."

"Well, Joe said you are not to worry about it. If he missed something, it'll be under his personal warranty."

She shook her head. "He's too good to me. I don't know what I'd do without him."

"Sounds like you have a lot of good friends who want to help...like the one on the phone."

"She's not really a friend—well, she used to be, but today she was pumping me for information. She's desperate to get in with a certain group of people, which just happens to be led by another of my ex-friends."

"Ex? That sounds ominous."

"Not really. The three of us were friends in high school—Laurie, Angie, and me. We did everything together. I think Laurie and I were closer. Angie was always...more competitive." She shrugged one shoulder. "Somehow, we managed to fall for the same guys."

"Let me guess. Angie didn't like it when *you* got the guy, and you usually got the guy."

"Well, yes...it did seem to happen that way a lot. But Angie's beautiful. She has incredible blue eyes and long blonde hair. She was fun and popular." Rafaela frowned. "I never understood why a guy would choose me over her."

A wry smile spread over Brett's lips and he shook his head. "You don't understand. Well, allow me to explain." He leaned forward over the arm of the chaise. Closer, so close the flecks in his hazel eyes became a deep shade of smoky green. "Your hair is like a curtain of black silk. It shimmers and moves like something alive and makes me want to run my fingers through it. And your eyes—no, they're not blue like your friend's—they're warm and dark, like a summer night. They make me think things I shouldn't. Your skin looks so smooth and creamy. I want to touch it just to make sure it's real." He leaned even closer and slid his finger down her cheek.

Rafaela's breath caught. She'd been holding it and now she was breathless and slightly dizzy.

"And if that's not enough to help you understand, there's more. You have an air of calm strength. A sense of purpose and certainty, of where you're going and what you are about."

"I sound like someone driven. That's not very appealing." Her words came out just above a whisper.

Brett flashed a white smile that struck a burning arrow straight through her heart. If he didn't turn that weapon down a notch or two, she'd be putty in his hands.

"There's nothing a man likes more than a challenge."

"Is that how you see me? As a challenge?"

Brett smiled at her edgy tone. "No, Rafaela. I see you as a mystery. An intriguing, beautiful mystery."

He was so close. If she leaned forward just a bit, their lips would touch. She hesitated, knowing she was in too deep, and wondering if she cared.

Brett moved forward. His lips were warm and firm and citrusy—like the drink in his hand. Rafaela felt awkward, out of her element. While she held still, Brett gripped her chin with two fingers and nudged her mouth to fit his.

The kiss felt so right. So easy. And far too short.

Brett leaned back and ran his thumb over her damp lips. "Wow."

"Wow good or wow weird?" Was that breathy, husky voice really hers?

"Wow as in we have *some* kind of chemistry. Chemistry and mystery. A double punch."

A double punch all right. Rafaela's senses tilted. She still felt his lips on hers. Still tasted the citrus sweetness, savored the warmth and strength. But guilt wormed its way in. How could she kiss a man she'd barely known a few days? Why was he moving so fast, determined to become a part of her family circle?

"Mama says dinner is ready." Sofia stood in the open French doors.

Rafaela jerked away as if Brett were fire.

How much had her sister seen? The knowing smirk flirting over Sofia's lips told Rafaela she'd seen enough, maybe even too much.

Great! Now I'm a bad influence on my baby sister.

Brett seemed completely at ease. He handed his glass to Rafaela then scooped her into his arms.

"I'm perfectly capable of walking."

He ignored her protest. "Of course you are. But I'm starving and I don't want to wait for you to hobble across the patio on those crutches. I already smell something delicious just waiting for me."

Rafaela wanted to be frustrated, to show disapproval, but the distinctive scent of fajitas drifted through the air. Bell peppers, onions, and delicately seasoned chicken. Rafaela's favorite and one of her mother's best dishes. Her stomach cramped slightly, reminding her that she hadn't eaten all day. *OK. You win this round Mr. Fraser, but I'm going to be ready for the next one…and I'll have a full stomach.*

Sofia followed them inside.

Brett eased Rafaela into a chair and chose the one next to her.

Sofia sat across from them, still wearing her wide smile.

Mama asked Brett to say grace.

Showing no signs of discomfort at the request, he bowed his head. His deep voice echoed across their table, but Rafaela barely heard the words. They knew so little about him. Was he a faithful man? Where had his spiritual journey taken him?

Her mother beamed as Brett dipped chicken fajita mixture onto her homemade tortillas, and Sofia smiled when he tasted the hot salsa. He had slipped so easily into their lives. Perhaps Rafaela should learn more about this charismatic man and put her insecurities about their obvious attraction on the back burner. After all, wasn't her goal to protect her family? What better way than to dive into the mystery of Brett Fraser? To find out what made him tick, and why he was so determined to become a part of their lives. Because Rafaela didn't believe for one second that mutual attraction was his only motive, even if the two of them *did* have the undeniable double punch of chemistry and mystery.

"Mija, I heard your phone ring. Is everything OK with the shop?"

Her mother's quietly spoken question caught

Rafaela off guard.

"Yes, it's fine." Rafaela shrugged one shoulder. "Laurie wanted to know if she could help."

Lucia lowered her fork. "Oh, dear, is she still spying for Angie?"

"Spying? You didn't mention anything about spying," Brett murmured.

Rafaela gave Brett a pointed glance. "I didn't get the chance. I was distracted."

A little smile tilted one corner of his mouth. "Oh, yeah. A very nice distraction."

Across the table, Sofia giggled and ducked her head. So her little sister had seen the kiss.

Rather than draw their mother's attention to Sofia's overreaction, Rafaela launched into an explanation of her relationship with her high school friends. "I told you Angie was very competitive. I didn't realize how deep that streak ran until she returned from college. By then I was running my father's gallery and Angie, who had never shown any interest in art, opened her own gallery just down the street."

"I see."

"Unfortunately for us," Lucia said with a shake of her head, "She's done surprisingly well."

"Yes. Angie has a flair for presentation and an eye for good art. If she wasn't determined to do better than me at everything, I'd value her entrance into the coalition of plaza shop owners. But she's so set on causing problems for me that I find it difficult to even speak to her."

"So she sends Laurie to ask questions for her." Brett frowned. "Why is Laurie so willing to do her bidding?"

"It's kind of sad, really. Laurie's marriage has hit some rocky ground. Her husband's job provides very well for them, but he's gone a lot. Laurie's decided the only way she can fill the emptiness in her life is to join the social set at the country club and—"

"Angie is the leader of that group."

Rafaela smiled. Brett's mind worked so quickly. He connected the dots quicker than anyone she'd ever met.

"Exactly. Laurie's intrusive questions have always been annoying, but they never caused me any real concern. But ever since Emilio started his new line of wood carvings, her intrusions have been constant. I have the feeling Angie's new goal is to steal Emilio away from me."

"Can she do that?"

"Not really. Emilio and I have been friends since we were kids. He's more like a brother or a cousin than a customer. But…" She hesitated.

"But?"

"Well, I care about Emilio. I want what's best for him. If it reaches the point where I think Angie can do more for him, I'll encourage him to go to her."

Brett's brow knitted but he remained silent, giving her another reason to appreciate him.

She could almost see him mentally chalking off the impediments that might prevent her from presenting Emilio's work. Print and radio ads. Posters and mailings. Refreshments and invitations. Rafaela could barely afford to pay her rent. All of the necessary expenses for a new artist showing would break her.

On the other hand, Angie's family had deep pockets. They could provide all the exposure Emilio's new line needed.

Tanya Stowe

"The right presentation is the key to the successful launch of a new line." Brett nodded in agreement. "Troy and Eliza are struggling with that decision right now."

"Troy and Eliza Madrigal?" Rafaela could not conceal her amazement. The Madrigals were stars in the art world. Her mind reeled at the thought that they might have to struggle with anything.

Brett, on the other hand, knew them intimately. They were his close friends and associates. The chasm between Rafaela's world and his suddenly loomed, gaping wide. Her question and all her thoughts slipped into that deep crevice, leaving her silent.

Fortunately, her mother didn't appear to have the same problem. "I can't imagine the Madrigals having to struggle over anything."

A wry smile slipped over Brett's lips. "Trust me; Eliza and Troy have had their share of real life issues." His smile and quiet tone reminded Rafaela of his troubled past. For the first time, she wondered about the details of the scandal that caused him to resign from his position at the Fallon School of Art.

"But what's troubling Eliza and Troy most right now is a new matter. They've collaborated on a piece, a whole new line of work combining glass and wood. Troy says it's unique and quite extraordinary, and he wants a new agent. Eliza's old agent expects to represent them, but he and Troy have never seen eye to eye. Troy feels they should choose a *new* agent to represent their *new* work. Eliza, of course, feels an obligation to her old agent and the gallery that gave her a start, not to mention the fact that she's done quite well financially. The whole issue has created quite a stir in their household."

"Why would they change if the agent's done well for her?"

"Let's just say, Troy doesn't feel he'll put as much effort into their combined work as he was willing to put into Eliza's."

"Oh, I see." Rafaela remembered a magazine picture of Eliza Madrigal—a petite redhead with an amazing peaches-and-cream complexion and brown eyes that seemed warm and welcoming. Her features were distinctive and very attractive. Apparently, her agent agreed.

"Wood and glass." Her mother's musing tone broke into her own thoughts. "That would take quite a bit of skill. How did they keep the glass's heat from setting the wood ablaze?"

"I haven't a clue, but if anyone could do it, Troy could. He's brilliant."

"I'd love to see it." Rafaela finally found her voice again.

Brett nodded and met her gaze. "So would I."

He gave a slight nod of appreciation, and her heart did a little flip—one more notch in the many ways they connected. Those links and similarities thrilled and frightened her at the same time.

"Unfortunately, Troy is keeping the work under tight wraps. No one has seen it yet, but I'm sure when he releases it, I'll get a first glimpse. I'll make sure you do, too."

Rafaela smiled. Pleasure burst through her like sunshine on a shaded meadow. Yes, life with Brett Fraser could be brighter, bigger and full of pleasures, some she hadn't even begun to sample.

Sofia popped up from her chair. "It's getting dark. I'm going to paint." She spun and headed for the door.

"Wait a minute..." Brett looked at Rafaela then at Sofia, with a question in his gaze. "Shouldn't you help with the dishes? Your mother spent the whole day on her feet at the gallery, and then prepared this wonderful meal from scratch. The least you and I can do is wash up."

"Oh, no, I can't let you do the dishes." Mama surged to her feet.

And Sofia stood frozen, waiting, obviously surprised that someone even dared to include her in the cleanup crew.

Rafaela almost laughed out loud at both their responses, but curiosity kept her silent. Who would win the battle?

"There's no question about 'letting me,' Lucia. I won't eat if I can't earn my way. If you don't let me lend a hand, I won't be coming back." He said it with all seriousness.

His expression stifled the little giggle threatening to escape the fingers pressed against Rafaela's lips. Torn between the pleasure of his company and the certainty in his demand to help, her mother backed down.

"Well, I guess it's all right to help."

"All right then. Sofia, let's get busy."

Brett didn't even spare Sofia a glance. He just motioned her into action and rose to stack the dishes.

Rafaela held her breath.

Sofia stood indecisively at the door.

Their mother had never expected much help from her youngest child. Since the onset of Sofia's illness, nothing was demanded.

Rafaela seriously doubted her sister even knew how to do the dishes. What's more, Sofia would likely protest or at the very least, sulk her way out of the simple chore.

But to Rafaela's shock and amazement, Sofia shrugged and headed across the room to help.

Rafaela's lips parted.

Yes, life with Brett Fraser was definitely bigger, brighter, and better.

~*~

"You know, Sofia, if you want to go paint now, I can finish up."

The young girl paused as she wiped a skillet dry, and stared at Brett.

He'd cajoled Lucia into resting while he and Sofia finished up the pots and pans.

Rafaela sat on a stool, elbows on the breakfast bar, chin in hand. Her eyes crinkled and a slight smile played about her lips as she listened to her sister chatter. With her guard down, her expression seemed so innocent, so open and young.

Brett could barely keep his focus on the job at hand. His gaze strayed back to the fetching picture every few minutes.

"I get it." Sofia smirked. "You want to be alone with my sister."

Sofia's more clever than I thought. He studied her too-slender form and the doe-like eyes now fixed on him with a wise expression. She continually surprised him, and he vowed not to underestimate her again. "I'd like nothing better than to spend more time with your sister. But I have another reason for sending you away. I want to see that lovely painting finished."

Her smile turned to a frown. "It'll never be

finished. At least not the way I've painted it."

"Why not?"

"My hands. I can't paint hands. They look funky. I'll just have to stick with still life. Sunsets and flowers."

"I thought your body form looked well-proportioned."

"My father would have laughed at it." She shook her head and looked away, avoiding his gaze.

"Not laughed, surely. He wouldn't expect your work to equal his. It takes a lot of training to perfect the human form."

"He would have laughed," Sofia said with firm conviction.

Brett glanced at Rafaela. She gave a non-committal shrug, but that shuttered look she'd shed for a little while slid over her features again. Brett remembered Lucia's description of her husband and wondered just how much influence Rafael de Silva had cast over his wife and daughters.

Young talent like Sofia's needed nurturing and instruction—not criticism. With training, the young woman could become a superb talent. In fact, she was a perfect candidate for the Fallon School of Art.

That was an excellent idea. One he'd have to give more consideration. He finished the dishes and drained the water.

Sofia put soap in the dishwasher and punched the start button. She was a perfect candidate for the school, and the school would be good for her.

Shivers traveled up his spine, and he wondered if it wasn't God's hand guiding him once again. But he didn't mention his idea just yet. First of all, he didn't like how Rafaela's lips had tightened or how both girls refused to meet his gaze. It seemed that the mention of their father had brought back too many memories. But more importantly, he didn't want to mention his own association with the Fallon School of Art. They might start asking questions he wasn't prepared to answer.

"The dishwasher is leaking!" Sofia's exclamation broke Brett's thoughts and almost brought Rafaela to her feet.

"Don't put any weight on that foot. I'll get it."

Pulling Sofia away from the growing puddle, he punched the stop button. "Sofia, grab the mop for me."

She ran out of the room.

"Great! That's all I need. One more repair bill." Rafaela's woeful tone gave Brett pause.

"I'll take a look. More than likely it's something simple. And even if it's not, I'll probably be able to save you a repair bill."

"You think you can fix our dishwasher?" Her disdainful tone was almost insulting.

"No, I don't think I can, Rafaela. I know I can."

8

Sofia hurried in, carrying a bucket and mop.

Lucia followed closely behind. "What's this? The dishwasher is broken?"

Brett raised his hands. "Let's not panic yet. It's probably something simple. I'm just about to take a look." He took the bucket. "Sofia, why don't you go paint? Lucia, go on back to what you were doing and I'll handle this. If I need you, I'll call you."

She glanced once at Rafaela, who to Brett's delight, shrugged again. Maybe his guarded, petite, little fortress was beginning to trust a little.

"At least, let me clean this up," Lucia said.

Brett smiled at the older woman. "I can't get in there and look at what's wrong until the water is gone. Why should both of us be detained? Let me do this. I'll call you if I need you."

Heaving a heavy sigh she turned. "You win, but somehow it doesn't feel right."

When she and Sofia had left the room, Rafaela sent him a piercing glare. "All right, Mr. Fix-it man, let's see what you can do."

Her acerbic tone didn't dampen his good humor. "Oh, ye of little faith."

Grinning, he mopped the water and scooted the heavy machine out of its nook. "So what makes you think I'm not capable of some simple repairs?"

"Let's just say you didn't get to be Daniel Fallon's

protégé fixing dishwashers."

He eased down on the already dry tiles. "So you think I was born with a silver spoon in my mouth."

"When I first read about you in the paper, I did wonder why such a young man was chosen to head up a prestigious school."

The black water hose at the back of the machine was bleached white with age, dry and dripping a steady rivulet of water from a wide crack.

"And I couldn't possibly have earned the position on the basis of my qualifications. It had to be handed to me because of my connections, right?" Brett inched the machine out further so he could reach the hose connections.

"It's not an illogical assumption. It happens more often than not."

"It might not be illogical but it's totally wrong." He tried to keep resentment out of his tone but wasn't completely successful. "Do you have a screwdriver?" Perhaps the change of subject would conceal his frustration.

"Under the sink. There should be small tool box with some tools."

He didn't spare her a glance as he pulled out the small, old-fashioned metal box and fished out the screwdriver. "My father was a general contractor. I spent my summers working for him. Even put myself through school that way."

"A contractor—like with a hammer and nails?"

He made no reply while he unscrewed the metal band clamps holding the damaged hose in place. After pulling it loose, he held it out for Rafaela to see. "Yes." His simple gesture and statement made a huge point.

"That's it? A cracked hose?"

"Looks like it. The cold-water hose is in pretty bad shape too. I'll take this in tomorrow and find replacements for both of them." He sent her another pointed look, waiting.

A slight smile played about her lips. "I don't know what to say."

"How about 'Thank you, Brett. I'll look forward to seeing you tomorrow.'"

"Thank you. I really do appreciate your help." She didn't say she wanted to see him again. But that ghost of a smile still played around her lips. She was teasing him, taunting, and he liked it.

Smiling, he rose to his feet, pushed the dishwasher back in place, and brushed off his jeans. "Hope it's OK if those dishes sit in there overnight. It's getting late and I want to see Sofia's progress."

Not waiting for a response, he hurried out the French doors. But he caught her slightly surprised and befuddled expression through the glass before he turned the corner of the house. Good. He'd gladly keep Rafaela guessing about his motives and methods. He liked to tease back.

The sun had already dipped behind the hill. Dusk surrounded them like a soft, furry blanket.

Sofia wiped her brushes on a cloth and placed them in her box while Brett silently studied her painting.

He had to agree. The hands were slightly out of proportion, but the body shape she'd painted was excellent. In fact, more than excellent. The slender shape in the painting bordered on dangerously thin, which told Brett that Sofia was very aware of her true body image. Another thought-provoking realization about the teenager and her illness. Most people suffering from anorexia had a warped body image. But Sofia seemed well aware of her unhealthy state. Brett took that as a good sign.

He made a point of telling Sofia how realistic her body shape appeared. "The hands need a little work. With a little instruction you'll improve those quickly."

She murmured her thanks, but the slight color tinting her cheeks told him how much she cared.

She didn't meet his gaze but kept her focus on her busy hands. "I did like you said. I looked you up. You do know a lot about art." She hesitated. "Would I be a good person for your school?"

So Sofia was interested. Apparently, Rafaela was the only member of her family opposed to the idea of her sister attending the Fallon School of Art. Even Lucia was intrigued by the idea. Still, he needed to tread carefully. He didn't want to cause dissension between Rafaela and her family. "Yes. I think you would be an excellent student."

Sofia closed her painter's box and reached for the painting. Brett took the heavy canvas from her, and she folded the easel before they headed back toward the house.

"But your school is very expensive."

"First of all, Sofia, it's not my school. Not anymore. I left it in much better hands than mine. But I do know there are scholarships available. Lara Fallon is very sincere in her desire to help young artists like you."

"You think I'd have a chance?"

"Yes. You'd have a very good chance." He stopped and turned to face her. "In fact, Sofia, think about this very carefully. If you apply, you'll probably qualify, and then you and your mother would be on your way. Would you be ready to go?"

Her gaze widened. She looked around the grounds and back at the broken fence. Doubt furrowed her brow.

"It would be a great chance, Sofia. The only thing stopping you would be you." He spoke so quietly, he wasn't sure she heard the words until she gave a slight nod of her head.

"I'll do what you say, Brett. I'll think about it...a lot."

~*~

How does he do that?

Rafaela stared at the French Doors where Brett had exited. *No matter how well I think I handle our conversations, he always manages to leave me guessing...or wondering...or daydreaming. Like right now.* What was it about him that kept her so intrigued, well, besides his quick wit and magazine-cover good looks? Rafaela smiled at her own wry thoughts. Who wouldn't be intrigued? Brett had everything. Any normal woman would be head over heels, but Rafaela couldn't shake the feeling that something wasn't quite right. *Maybe it's me who has the problem. Maybe I'm too untrusting and suspicious.*

She shook her head. It had been so long since she'd had a real relationship; she couldn't judge her own responses anymore. But she valued truth, even when it applied to her own motives or failures. And the only way to know the truth was to continue her quest to know the man.

Brett and Sofia returned. Her sister was laughing and something inside Rafaela melted. Laughter had been missing from Sofia's life for too long. No matter what the future held, Rafaela would be forever thankful for the way Brett had brought light into the dark corners of Sofia's heart.

Her mother joined them, asking about the dishwasher. She, Brett, and Sofia chatted for a few moments.

Already feeling tender toward Brett, Rafaela couldn't help but study the sight of them gathered around her mother's kitchen sink. With the soft, golden light flowing over them and her mother's colorful Santa Fe crockery surrounding them, they seemed posed, like a lovely painting. Almost like a family. Rafaela was stunned by how deeply the image buried itself in her soul. *If only.*

"Well, it's getting late. I should let you ladies have your beauty rest."

Brett's joke sufficiently stomped on her wishful thoughts.

Lucia wrapped the broken dishwasher parts in a plastic bag.

Rafaela rose from her spot on the breakfast barstool. Stiff, sore muscles let her know how long she'd been sitting and a small exclamation of surprise escaped.

Brett was by her side instantly. "Are you hurting? Do you need help?"

"No, no I'm fine. What I need is to move. I'll walk you to your car."

He handed her the crutches, grabbed the bag of parts, and followed her limping gait out the French doors.

The night air was warm. Stars sparkled in a black velvet sky. Pine floated on the air and mixed with the sweet scent of her mother's bougainvillea climbing the courtyard wall. Everything felt soft and gentle.

Rafaela paused, waiting for Brett to catch up.

"So how does someone with your mad repair skills end up in the art world? Shouldn't you have been an architect or something?"

Brett slowed his gait to match Rafaela's limp. "My mother was an art professor at the local college."

"Wow. Your parents had very different personalities."

"Tell me about it. They divorced when I was in junior high."

Rafaela halted. "I'm sorry. I didn't mean to bring up bad memories." Even though she wanted to discover more about Brett, she spoke the truth. Harsh memories didn't belong here, not in this gentle night full of beauty and peace.

Brett opened his car door, releasing a blast of hot air, and tossed the bag onto the floorboard. "Don't worry about it. Their parting happened so long ago, it doesn't hurt anymore. And honestly, they fought so much that it was almost a relief when they went their separate ways. They were much better friends afterwards."

He crossed his arms over the top of the low-slung sport's car door and leaned toward her. "And I like to think I'm a good blend. I used all I learned about business and management and focused those skills in the much-needed art world. It showcased the best of my multi-sided personality." He flashed that wry little grin he used with all his self-mocking statements.

He meant it to disarm and distract, but Rafaela wasn't put off. She sensed some deeper emotion behind his teasing.

"What was your major in college?"

Did he hesitate or was it a trick of the moonlight?

"Non-profit corporations and their management."

To her surprise, he didn't make a joke, and a piece of the Brett Fraser puzzle slipped into place.

"And I imagine you were at the top of your class. That's how you attracted Daniel Fallon's attention and became the director of the Fallon School of Art."

"Yes. It's also how I blew it and almost turned the grand opening into a disaster."

She paused, waiting, hoping he would tell her more, explain the details, maybe reveal the secrets she sensed he was holding back. But he didn't. Instead he kept his gaze focused on the black shadows of the distant mountains, not even daring to look at her.

Rafaela didn't fear the truth, and she refused to back down from it, even on a night like this. "Why are you doing this, Brett?" Her tone was full of piercing honesty. "Why are you going so far out of your way for me and my family?"

Finally he looked at her. By the silver light of the moon, she could see his hazel eyes. They were open and sincere.

"I'm attracted to you, Rafaela. I thought I made that pretty apparent, but if you're not sure, I'll be glad to demonstrate it once more." Joking again and flashing that telltale grin to go along with it.

But she wouldn't be put off. "I'm attracted to you, too, but I'm not living my life and focusing every day around your needs. What you're doing goes above and beyond."

"Yes."

His heavy sigh gave her hope that maybe he would finally give her a complete answer.

"Yes, you're right." He sighed again. "I have done a few simple things for you, but each time I've enjoyed the pleasure of your company. To me, it's a win/win situation, Rafaela. I can do things for you that you need, and you, well, in case you didn't notice, my life lately has been empty. I've been wandering for months and now...now my life suddenly has purpose. I think I've been led here, Rafaela. You say I've helped you, but the truth is, you've helped me. I need you."

At last. True words. She could see the honesty in his expression, in the hesitancy of his admission, even in the lack of his teasing smile. The reality of his statement sent shivers up her arms and spine. Nothing ever felt or sounded so right. He *had* been led here. She knew it, felt it in every bone of her body. For his good or hers, or maybe both. She didn't know, but she knew for certain that God had sent Brett Fraser into her life.

The rightness of it, the soft moonlight, his teasing smile and the dark sincerity of his green-tinted eyes drew her to him like a moth to silver light. Tucking her crutches under her arms, she cupped his face with her hands and drew his lips down to hers.

They felt like honey, smooth and tender and oh-so-perfect.

"I believe you, Brett, right or wrong. I believe you."

~*~

Aaron Pomeroy's website was thorough. His real estate business dealt in commercial properties, offices, apartments, and industrial complexes. From what Brett could tell, the man was well-fixed financially, and his connections and recommendations came from some very influential New Mexico residents. But a website only told half the story. Brett wouldn't find the real Aaron Pomeroy there.

To purchase the supplies, he needed to repair the dishwasher and the off-kilter front gates, Brett purposely chose small, independent, and locally owned hardware stores. He started conversations with the owners, asking for a recommendation of a good real estate agent for commercial property. All of them recognized Pomeroy's name. Some had dealings with him, others just knew the name. Those who knew Pomeroy gave Brett mixed reactions about the man, but nothing substantial to point Brett in any direction.

He left the last store feeling as if he'd hit a brick wall. And then an idea came to him. Maybe the idea bordered on desperation. It might even get him into trouble, but once the thought took root, he couldn't shake it.

After making his last purchase, he sat in his car, looked up the number for Pomeroy's office, and dialed. Thankfully, he'd long since put a block on his cellphone so that it remained anonymous to caller ID.

"Mr. Pomeroy's office." The woman's voice sounded rich, low, and sexy.

Brett took a deep breath. "Tell Pomeroy Louis Ferone needs to speak to him."

"Oh. Mr. Ferone, I thought—" The receptionist broke off in total confusion.

Bingo. The woman had every right to be confused. Louis Ferone was in jail.

"Mr. Pomeroy is out of the office, Mr. Ferone. Can I take a message?"

"No. I'll call back. In fact, don't even mention that I called. I'll contact him later."

Brett clicked off. As underhanded as it had been, he had established a connection between Pomeroy and the man serving time in jail for transporting illegally obtained Chaco pottery.

He released his breath.

Pomeroy and Ferone knew each other or at least had some business dealings. Their connection could be legal. In fact, their only connection could simply be Pomeroy's brokering of the Chaco pottery he sold for Rafaela.

But if Brett were a betting man, he'd bet a good pile of money that there was more to it. Pomeroy had rubbed him the wrong way right from the beginning, and if Brett had learned anything from his experience in Sedona, it was to trust his instincts. That meant he needed help. Only one person could give him the help he needed. Alexander Summers.

Alex had been the instrument of Brett's destruction. At least, he'd been the catalyst that tumbled Brett's house of cards into a messy pile. A world-renowned Flamenco player, the man had been hired by Troy to entertain at the school's opening ceremonies.

Alex also worked undercover for the I.C.E. They'd asked him to investigate the school to determine if anyone was involved in shipping black market artifacts out of the country. Alex accomplished his task, but he hadn't counted on falling in love with Lara Fallon, Brett's closest friend. Alex worked hard to prove the school and all of them innocent.

What Alex had not been able to do was to clear Brett's conscience. No matter how he looked at it, he felt responsible. If he'd been more vigilant, less worried about pleasing others—maybe even less ambitious and determined to take care of everything himself.

That thought sent him searching for Alex Summers's number. Brett wasn't about to repeat his mistake. He was going to call in the big dogs.

"Hello." Summers's rich voice echoed over the phone, classical Spanish guitar music playing in the background. Another reason Brett had a hard time liking the guy. Summers had a huge, fawning, female following, and he owned a million-dollar guitar with its own legend of lost lovers.

La Guitarra's legend told of two lovers, Juan and Lucia. Juan played the gypsy music of his people and Lucia danced. Everyone who saw them got caught in the spell of La Guitarra's magic. Later, Juan and Lucia were separated by a villainous nobleman determined to possess Lucia. Juan swore never to play La Guitarra until he found his lost love.

The legend had enough mystery and romance to capture any woman's heart, not that Summers needed La Guitarra's magic to win a woman. He had enough magnetism on his own. Obviously. He'd won the heart of Lara Fallon.

And that was the other reason Brett had resisted Summers's help in the beginning. Brett and Lara had an "understanding" before Summers stepped into their lives. Last Brett heard, Lara and Alex were engaged to be married.

In all honesty, Brett harbored no ill feelings. What Brett had thought was love, was affection and a deep, abiding friendship. Now that he'd met Rafaela, he realized how wrong he'd been about his feelings for Lara. They paled in comparison to what he felt for Rafaela. She consumed him. He thought of her when he first woke in the morning and when he closed his eyes at night. He wanted to know everything about her, to protect her and to help her in any and every way. For that reason, he wasn't going to allow his male pride to get in his way.

"Alex. This is Brett Fraser."

"Fraser." Surprise brought a questioning tone into Alex's simple greeting. "It's good to hear from you. Lara's been worried. She hasn't heard from you in a while."

"Yes, I know. I'm sorry about that. I'm in Santa Fe."

"Santa Fe. Well, that's not so far away. Lara didn't know how to reach you to send you an invitation to our wedding."

Brett smiled. Alex was one of the more subtle men Brett had ever met, and the sharpest. The mention of the wedding was purposeful, a way to probe how Brett felt. He was more than happy to put Alex's mind to rest.

"It's about time you set a date. I thought you might wait so long Lara'd slip away." Brett grinned as he spoke the words.

"Uhhh, no. That would not have happened."

Brett heard the smile in Alex's tone, but also knew the words were true. Summers was not the type of man to let anything slip from his grasp, especially not the best things.

Hopefully, Brett would be that kind of man, also. "I still don't have an address but tell me the date and I'll be there with bells on."

"October. After the school opens and things settle down."

"Sounds perfect. I'll do my very best. In the

meantime, I need to talk to you about something." Brett explained the situation with Pomeroy and the de Silvas. Even about his call to Pomeroy's office.

Alex waited until Brett completely finished before he spoke. "It does sound like you've found something worth looking into. I'll contact my friends at I.C.E. They'll take it from there. In the meantime, call Lara and Troy. They're worried about you."

"I will. Thanks."

"And, Brett...be careful. If these men are involved, they're dangerous. They almost shot Lara. They're willing to kill to get what they want."

9

"Wait! You can't fix that!"

Sofia's exclamation startled Brett so much he jumped back from the tilted front gate.

Rafaela couldn't help laughing at the completely befuddled expression on his face.

She'd been doing that a lot in the past two weeks. Smiling and laughing. Enjoying life. And she owed it all to the man standing in front of her, shaking his head.

"Why *can't* I fix this gate? It's too beautiful to leave in disrepair."

"It's beautiful the way it is. It has such character...such..."

Brett gave a shrug. "It needs to be repaired before it falls off completely."

"But..." Sofia began.

"I have an idea." Rafaela eased down on her crutches. "How about you use my cellphone to take a picture of it? Then you can paint it and preserve it forever and Brett can go ahead with his repairs."

The young artist's face brightened. "It would be better if I could sketch it. That way I'll have the colors fixed in my mind." She said the last on a hopeful note, her eyebrows raised in question. She paused, waiting for Brett's response.

"Sounds good to me. I'll work on the fence."

Sofia gave Brett a quick hug and dashed off in the direction of the house.

Rafaela would be forever thankful for the impact he had on her young sister. In a short two weeks, Sofia had gained a new outlook—one with smiles and laughter. Much like her older sister.

What a difference one man could make, not only with their emotions, but on their home as well. He'd offered to do some small repairs around the rancho. Her mother agreed, but only if he stayed in the studio so she could pay him with dinner every night. It seemed the perfect solution, and the place had never looked better, not even when her father had been alive. Just like the rest of her family, the de Silva rancho seemed to glow and blossom under Brett's tender care.

He gathered his tools into a brown cardboard box and headed toward the back fence. He flashed a grin. "Changing my plans is worth it if I get a response like that every time."

"I agree."

As he passed her, he winked. "I'll be slaving away all by my lonesome out back if you decide you need some company."

"I have to finish the gallery's bookkeeping, but I'll send Sofia as soon as she's done with her sketch." Rafaela smiled at her quick-witted response.

Brett chuckled. "Not quite what I had in mind but enjoyable just the same."

Shouldering the box of tools, he moved out of sight, and she watched until he was gone. Then she settled on the chaise with her laptop and tried hard to concentrate on her work.

Quite some time later, she finished the gallery's monthly bills. Across the way, Sofia flipped her sketchbook closed and stretched as she sauntered toward her sister.

"Finished already?" Rafaela hiked one eyebrow. "That must have been a quick job."

"Not quick but easy. The gates are sooooo beautiful. Want to see?"

Rafaela tried not to show her surprise. She'd not been allowed to view her sister's work in months. "Yes." She murmured a quick agreement before Sofia could change her mind.

Sofia flipped open the book and handed it over. The penciled drawing leapt off the page. The outlines of the form were simple, light and delicate, like shadows of the real thing, but the details were dark and perfect. Sofia possessed an impeccable eye for specifics. The cracked wood grain. The rusted hinge. The chipped blue paint. Even in black and white the image seemed colorful.

"You're right. The gate is beautiful when viewed through your eyes, Sofia. It will be a stunning painting."

"Do you really think so?"

"Yes, I do. I would love to hang it in the gallery. It would pull people off the street and into the shop."

Sofia's gaze widened in surprise. "Would you really hang it?"

Rafaela hesitated. "Only if you wanted me to, of course."

"Are you kidding? That would be great." Her face clouded. "But first I need to paint it, and then we'll see. My sketches are always better than the real thing."

"Who said? Did Brett tell you that?"

"No, Papa did."

Rafaela felt a catch in her breath. Their perfectionist father had often been a harsh critic. "That was a long time ago, Sofia. You were very young then.

Your work has grown a lot."

"That's true. Brett thinks I'm talented."

"Brett's a very good judge. You should listen to him."

Sofia nodded. "I think I'll go show this to him and see what he says."

"Good idea."

Long after her sister had gone, Rafaela sat in silent contemplation. Almost immediately after their father's death, creditors had started hounding them. Rafaela was forced to face the ugly side of their father's nature early in her grief—forced to deal with his shortcomings and weaknesses. Those events had definitely changed her feelings about her beloved father.

For years after his death, she resented him and his passionate, single-minded devotion to his art. After a while, though, she realized resentment and anger were a natural part of the grieving process. With a lot of prayer, she'd learned to forgive her father's harsh side and move on.

She'd never stopped to consider the impact the severe aspect of his personality had on her younger sister. But now, she saw her father's critical nature in a different light. Instead of feeling partly responsible for her sister's current state-of-mind, Rafaela began to wonder if those seeds had not been planted long ago and perhaps even more harshly since their father was so focused on perfection in art. Sofia may have been at the receiving end of much of that demanding side of his personality.

Rafaela had no doubt that had her father lived, he would have grown with Sofia, and his opinions of her work would have grown too. But death had brought all those possibilities to an abrupt halt and left her sister, her mother, and herself in limbo.

Somehow, the thought that the beginnings of Sofia's mental state may have been planted long ago made Rafaela feel less guilty, less responsible.

Sofia, their mother, even Rafaela—none of them needed to be bound to the past any longer.

Rafaela closed her eyes. *Thank You, Lord. Thank You for the gift of Brett in our lives at this time. I'll do my very best to move us forward, wherever that takes us.* With her eyes closed, the sun beat down on her. The late afternoon heat was almost unbearable. Gathering her books, she slid them in the bag she carried over her shoulder and hobbled into the kitchen.

Brett was working in this heat and would probably appreciate a cold drink. She'd become pretty handy with her crutches, so she set about brewing some fresh tea. When she finished, she poured the tea into a sealable pitcher, put lids on three glasses full of ice, tucked them all into her bag and headed toward the back fence.

Even before she rounded the corner, Sofia and Brett's voices rang out in the shimmering heat, discussing painting again. Brett never seemed to tire of answering Sofia's questions about her art. The solid *thunk* of bricks landing in the metal wheelbarrow Brett had brought out of the shed was interspersed into their conversation. Their chatter and the metal ping sounded normal and completely expected as they came into her view.

Brett had removed his shirt—obviously the heat had overwhelmed him. His suntanned torso rippled with taut muscles, and Rafaela's mouth went dry. Unprepared for the sight of his sweat-slicked six-pack, Rafaela stopped short, almost tumbling over her crutches as she looked away. Who would have thought such a slender body could pack so much power and strength? *Why, Lord? Why after all these years?* She'd avoided relationships and resisted every temptation thrown her way. But this man would be her undoing. He'd already conquered her emotions. Would he also defeat her self-control? *Did you send him to me to teach me humility, Lord?* The thought overwhelmed her. She looked up once more, basking in the sight of his lean shape and the warm smile he bestowed on her sister.

Yes. Definitely humbling to know he could wash away all her defenses by simply taking off his shirt. Until now, she'd believed herself above physical temptation. But with heat spreading into her cheeks, there was no denying how wrong she'd been. Brett Fraser was here to teach her humility.

"Hey, do you need help with that?"

Brett motioned for Sofia to hurry across and take the heavy bag.

"Thanks." Rafaela kept her eyes averted.

Sofia pulled apart the cloth handles and looked inside the bag. "She brought us something to drink, Brett. It's break time." Her sister moved toward the shade of a nearby Palo Verde tree.

Still reeling from her own thoughts, Rafaela stood her ground.

Sofia looked back over her shoulder. "You brought three glasses. Aren't you going to join us?"

"I-I was but I just realized the time. I promised Mama I'd mix the sopaipilla dough so it can rest before she gets home." She fled to the kitchen.

Still carrying Brett's image in her mind, she measured out the flour, shortening and milk for the traditional New Mexico fried pastry. By the time

Rafaela had cut in the shortening, mixed and set it aside to rest, her mother arrived home from work. She looked tired and a bit frazzled.

"Oh, good." Her mother soaped her hands at the sink. "You've got the dough started. I thought I'd stuff the sopaipillas with some of that tender pork I made last night. What do you think?"

"I think, Mama, that you look tired. Maybe we could just have leftovers."

"Are you kidding? I've been looking forward to this all day. Do you know how long it's been since I made stuffed sopaipillas?" Her mother slipped the apron over her head and hurried to the refrigerator. She had a spring to her step, an energy that had been missing when she walked in the door. Her mother loved to cook, and having Brett here to feed was adding sparkle to her day.

Brett had filled so many holes in their lives.

Someone to cook for.

Someone to talk to.

Someone to fall in love with...

There. The thought she'd been dancing around finally came to the surface. The real reason she feared Brett.

The mystery man who dropped from nowhere into their lives had better be all that he claimed to be, because Rafaela was dangerously close to falling in love with him. He'd brought laughter, hope and so much more. If he turned out to be something less, the disappointment would crush her. Discouragement had been such a constant companion for the last few years that she'd had difficulty climbing out from beneath its weight. If it happened again...

Rafaela chose not to think of it. Instead she

focused on her mother's happiness as she hummed in the kitchen, and Sofia's chatter, which Rafaela could still hear from the corner of the house, and the tingling glow that filled her each time the image of Brett's taut torso popped into her mind.

Thankfully, when dinner was ready, Brett had donned his shirt again. It made eating an easy affair, especially when he took a third helping of sopaipillas and her mother beamed with pleasure.

They were almost finished when Rafaela's cellphone rang.

"I'll get it for you." Sofia jumped up and dashed across the room to the desk. She had the phone back to Rafaela by the fourth ring.

"Hello." Her assistant Jan's voice echoed over the phone and Rafaela listened to her friend's strained tones, her heart growing heavy.

"No, Jan, we're fine. We'll take care of everything here. You just focus on taking care of your parents. All right. Call us if you need anything."

A heavy sigh eased out of her as she clicked off. "I can't believe this downward slide. First my ankle, then the truck, and now this."

A strange expression passed over Brett's features, an expression that turned into a deep frown.

"What is it, mija? What's happened to Jan?"

"She's all right, Mama, but her parent's home was broken into last night while they were out to dinner."

"Oh, dear," Her mother turned to Brett, who still wore a concerned frown. "Jan's parents are elderly. Every year she takes her vacation in Albuquerque to visit with them and to help catch up on doctor visits and household repairs. Her mother had a stroke and her father has heart issues."

"Yes, and this break-in has stressed them both out so much, Jan's afraid to leave them. She's not coming home as planned."

"I hope you told her to take as much time as she needed."

"Of course I did."

"Well, Aaron is in Albuquerque now. I'll call him later and ask him to check on Jan and her family. Maybe he can do something to help."

"I thought you said he was doing business in Phoenix." Brett's frown hadn't relaxed.

"Yes, but he had to fly into Albuquerque afterwards. He called and asked if I could drive his car to Albuquerque and pick him up next Monday."

"Now it looks as if you'll have to work in the gallery. I'm sorry. This puts more strain on you, Mama. I was hoping to go back to work next week. With Jan's help, I was certain I could manage the shop, but I'm not sure I can do it on my own."

"You don't need to do it on your own." Brett had stopped frowning but the tone of his voice still held a cautious tone. "I should be finished with the fence by the weekend. Next Monday I can drive you in and stick around to give you a hand."

Her mother and Sofia turned to her with hopeful expressions, but Rafaela ignored them. "I really appreciate the offer, but you've done so much already. We can't ask more of you."

"I thought we settled this, Rafaela. I don't have anything else taking center stage in my life. For now, I'm happy to be here. I'll help out at the gallery until you're on your feet, then we'll decide where to go from there."

We'll decide where to go from there.

Working together. Solving problems. Such a pleasant, hopeful thought. She liked the sound of it. He made it easy to agree. But their agreement didn't seem to ease whatever was troubling Brett. He tried to behave normally and insisted on helping with the cleanup, but afterwards, he begged off a game of Scrabble with Sofia and headed to the studio for an early bedtime.

Something was definitely wrong, and Rafaela couldn't let it rest. She followed him out to the courtyard, into the warm starlit night. Crickets stopped their chirping as they stood just outside the pattern of light falling through the French doors onto the courtyard flagstones.

"Brett. Tell me what's wrong."

He ran a hand around his neck. "I'm just a little tired tonight, that's all."

She shook her head. "You know all my secrets and problems but you won't share even one with me."

He twisted away and stared at the silver moon. "It's not my secret, Rafaela. I didn't want to say anything in front of Lucia or Sofia, and I really don't want to spoil your night but…"

"Go ahead, Brett. Tell me. Trying to guess what's wrong would spoil my night even more."

He released his breath slowly. "It's something you said."

"I said?"

"Yes. You couldn't believe this downward slide. Did you ever stop to consider that it might not be coincidental?"

"I don't understand. What do you mean?"

"Think about it. First you fall and injure your ankle. Two days later your truck breaks down for a reason your mechanic still can't figure out. And now your assistant can't make it back into work. That's too many inconvenient coincidences."

"Wait…are you saying someone is doing all these things?" She laughed. "That's crazy, Brett. I don't have enemies so desperate they're willing to hurt my business. Besides, no one could set up these things. They just happened."

"I don't agree." He jogged over to the main entrance where a wooden shoe rack sat outside the front door. Her mother had set her damaged running shoe on the rack the day of her accident. Brett picked it up and brought it back to the light of the French doors.

"Take a look at this shoe string. What do you see?"

She studied the item and, for the first time, noticed the clean cut through half of the string. She released it and looked up. "OK. It looks cut but that doesn't mean someone did it. The string was probably damaged in production. One strange incident doesn't make me the victim of a plot."

"That's the point. It's more than one strange incident. You said so yourself."

Rafaela shook her head. "Even if I agreed with you, I can't think of a single person who would want to hurt me."

"Are you sure? You said your friend Angie was more competitive than you realized. Are you certain she wouldn't use other measures to get what she wanted?"

Rafaela hesitated but only for a moment. "Yes, I'm sure. Angie's not desperate. She doesn't need to cause trouble for me. She's already winning. Her business is booming, and she knows I'm one step away from closing my doors."

10

For the second time in a week, Brett pulled the sunken light bulb out of the socket and stepped down from the ladder. Something was definitely wrong with the wiring. He'd have to contact the manager of the building so they could shut down the power. Either that or redesign Emilio's whole display.

The light was supposed to illuminate the artist's carefully crafted wooden carving of a weary Native American warrior. Embedded glass in strategic places drew in and reflected light, creating a magnificent and powerful display. Without light on the piece, however, those remarkable assets lost a great deal of impact.

In the two weeks that Brett had been helping Rafaela, he'd spent most of his days doing minor repairs, just as he had at the ranch. He'd also been available to help her build a few new displays and those chores had given him the most pleasure.

Rafaela was gifted with a true eye for color. His simple handyman skills allowed her to make the visions in her head come to reality. Together they'd created a more beautiful space.

Brett treasured every moment working with her, making new things from old and watching beauty take shape. In her own right, Rafaela was an artist too. That was the thing Brett loved most about the artistic world: watching the creation of something new. Better yet when the artist had shining dark hair and a rare but winsome smile.

Of course Rafaela's bum ankle had aggravated her and slowed her down. Fortunately, today was her freedom day. He expected her to return from her doctor's appointment any time without her crutches and ankle brace.

As happy as Brett was for her, a part of him almost dreaded the homecoming. Once her ankle was healed, he had no good excuse to stick around and makes himself useful. Rafaela's freedom day might be her "freedom from Brett" day, too.

Not that she seemed anxious for that to happen. Lately, Brett felt they'd reached new ground—an understanding and a mutual appreciation. But he also knew how much independence meant to Rafaela. It meant strength and healing, a return to life after so many years of mourning and struggling. He didn't want to take that away from her. He just wanted to share it.

No matter how much she demanded her independence, he would not be leaving until he was convinced she was safe. He hadn't been able to prove to Rafaela that she was in danger but he believed it. And he was not going anywhere until that little piece of mystery was resolved. Rafaela's downward slide might or might not be connected to his past and a dangerous black market operation stretching from Santa Fe to Sedona. That didn't seem as important anymore. All that really mattered was keeping his little family safe.

Brett almost tripped over the ladder. When did they become "his" family? How could he call them "his" and in the same thought consider leaving?

Leaning the ladder against the wall, he stared into

the distance. He was attracted to Rafaela and everything about her. He'd known that from the beginning. He'd asked her to let their relationship grow, and she had. Had it grown so much? Had his feelings for her tipped over that precarious cliff called love? He placed a hand on the ladder for balance. Just when he was on the verge of a monumental thought, his cellphone rang.

"Hey, Brett, this is Troy."

His friend's voice warmed Brett clear to the soul. He smiled broadly, although no one was there to see it. "Troy, I was about to give up. I thought maybe you didn't want to talk to me."

"Don't be crazy. We've missed you. I couldn't wait to call, but I was in the middle of some stressful negotiations with Eliza's agent."

"From the sounds of it, the talks didn't go so well."

"Depends on which side of the fence you're on. For me the outcome was great. Neville behaved just as I expected he would, so we'll be handling our own tour. He'll promote the showing in New York only. I'll arrange the rest of the tour. I think I have enough contacts to—" He broke off. "Sorry. I shouldn't bore you with my business details. I've just been preoccupied with this stuff."

"No problem. I was kind of busy myself."

"Busy? I thought you were on the road. Relaxing. 'Sabbatical-ing' or whatever you do on a sabbatical."

Brett chuckled. "I was. But lately I've been doing some manual labor, repairs. That kind of stuff."

"Do you need money?"

Brett warmed at the concern in his friend's voice. "No, I haven't lost my touch for that. I've got plenty put aside."

"Then why the repair work? Wait, do I sense some other motive? Exactly what kind of work are you doing?"

"Oh, a little of this and that."

"Right. Does this little of this and little of that have a name?"

Brett chuckled again. "As a matter of fact she does. Rafaela."

"I like the sound. Dark and exotic."

"She fits the bill, but she's also warm and passionate. Caring...smart..." He trailed off. The descriptions paled beside the real, living woman.

"Brett, my friend. This sounds pretty serious."

"It might be. It just might be."

"Well, then, Eliza and I have to meet her."

"I'd like that. In fact, I think I have a proposition you might find interesting. Have you considered doing an opening in Santa Fe?"

"No, I hadn't. But there's an artist there I've been following for some time. He's doing something very similar to what Eliza and I have created. His name is Emilio Gonzales, and I think he has a bright future."

Brett laughed out loud. "So do I. How would you like to give Emilio's career a lift and do a showing of your new work with his?"

"Well, that's intriguing. A good showing with a local artist would generate a lot of buzz. But that would depend completely on the gallery."

"I'd work with them, Troy. I promise it would be a good opening."

"Brett, if you're involved it will be. I know that."

A prickling at the back of Brett's throat made his voice scratchy. "I-I appreciate your confidence, Troy, especially after what happened."

"Brett, none of *us* blame you for what happened. You were the only one who lost confidence in you."

He cleared his throat. "Thanks. Just to show good faith, though, I'll take no fee and the gallery's sales commission will be reasonable, minus a few start-up costs."

"Now I'm really intrigued. What's the name of this place?"

"The de Silva Gallery."

"And is the owner of this gallery dark and exotic?"

"Yes, she is, but the place really is a gem. Rafaela has a gift."

"If she caught your attention, she has to be something special. Send me some pictures of the set-up. I'll talk with Eliza and see what we can work out."

~*~

"You what?" Rafaela's blood came to a quick boil. Her face burned as if someone had built a fire under her skin. She'd barely returned from her doctor's appointment when Brett hit her with his "wonderful" news. He couldn't even wait until she set down her things before he told her all about his arrangement.

Brett held up his hands, trying to placate her. "Don't go ballistic. Nothing's signed and sealed yet."

"It doesn't matter if it's finalized! How could you even suggest a business proposal without discussing it with me first? It's my business and my name on the line."

Brett shrugged. "Honestly, it just happened. Troy told me he wasn't allowing Eliza's agent to rep them and the idea popped out."

Rafaela knew Brett well enough to know he wasn't telling the truth. He had a hard time meeting her gaze. She tilted her head and narrowed her gaze. "Don't even go there. This idea's been rumbling around in your head for quite a while."

Brett shrugged. "Of course it has. I'm an idea man. But I didn't think it would come together. I was sure Troy and the agent would come to an understanding— at least a compromise. But then Troy said he was handling the tour, and it just felt right. I had to act on it."

"I thought you understood. I don't have the money for this." Her words came out more like a moan than a statement.

"That's why I negotiated a low commission and expenses to come out of the sale."

A pretty sweet deal. Rafaela studied him. "Troy agreed to that?"

"Yes—and you said you'd do anything for Emilio. This is a great opportunity. Troy and Eliza have already been following him."

"They've seen his work?"

Brett held up two fingers. "Scout's honor. Troy said he's been watching Emilio develop because they were working along the same lines."

"Wow. This could be the break he needs."

"Agreed. Not to mention what it will do for the gallery."

"*If* I can pull it together and pay for it."

Reaching across the space between them, Brett grasped her hands. "We can do it. Together we can make it happen."

A once-in-a-lifetime opportunity had landed in her lap, and she was berating its creator. What was wrong with her? She recognized the fact, but the heat in her blood hadn't quite gone below simmer. "You should have talked to me first, Brett."

"You're right. I should have. I'm sorry."

She released a sigh. "Maybe I overreacted a little. My father used to do things like this, arrange my life for me. I know you did what you thought best, but it makes me feel manipulated."

There it was again, that telltale darting of his gaze.

Her stomach wrenched and she narrowed her gaze. "What are you not telling me?"

He shrugged. "Maybe I acted impulsively too. I was a little off kilter when I left Sedona. I let them all down, and maybe I thought this would be a way to mend some bridges."

She pulled her hands free from his. "Maybe you'd better tell me exactly what happened."

He hesitated. "Yeah, I guess it's time."

Running a hand around the back of his neck, he pulled out the ladder and pointed to one of the steps. "Sit down. This could be a long story. You shouldn't put too much weight on that ankle first day out."

Rafaela pulled her long skirt tight around her bottom and poised on the slender step. Brett hooked an arm around the ladder and leaned in. Still, he couldn't seem to raise his gaze to hers. That simple gesture made Rafaela nervous.

"Daniel Fallon had an old enemy named Rupert Townsend. The man had a grudge against Daniel that went way back and had nothing to do with me. Still, Townsend used my inexperience and naiveté to get to Daniel.

"Somehow—I'm still not clear how—Townsend had connections with a black market group. They were shipping illegally obtained artifacts out of the country. Townsend blackmailed one of the shipping clerks at the school into using Fallon Enterprises as a cover. Of course, I.C.E. got wind of it, and we were all under investigation, right when we were soliciting donors for a grand opening. Thanks to Alex Summers, the plot was uncovered and the school was cleared of all wrongdoing. But the fact remains that the shipping fiasco was going on right under my nose and I missed it all."

She shook her head. "How could you have known?"

"There were suspicious events, missing checks, some threats. If I hadn't been so caught up with my own insecurities and worries..." He shook his head. "I should have asked questions, at the very least admitted to Daniel that I was in over my head and needed help. But I didn't."

"If Daniel Fallon is such a good businessman, why didn't he see the signs and send help?"

"He trusted me, put me in charge. I almost got my best friend shot, Rafaela. I put them all in danger because I didn't take action. Believe me; I won't make that mistake again."

She nodded slowly. So many things she hadn't understood about Brett finally fell into place. "Maybe that's why when you saw this opportunity for the gallery, you accepted without consulting me first."

He nodded, a wry smile slipping over his lips. "I wouldn't give myself an excuse quite that noble, but if you think it's true, I'll take it."

"Your past also explains why you see danger in every simple accident."

His smile faded. "I'll reserve my opinion on that

one. I won't fail the people I care about again."

The conviction in his tone should have filled Rafaela with confidence, made her feel secure. Instead, a thread of something icy slithered through her veins. "Is that why you're so determined to help my family? To prove you're not a failure?"

He winced. For the first time, he turned to face her. "I've asked God over and over again to make me useful. I believe He guided me here for that purpose, to be useful. I'm convinced of that."

He had been useful, more than useful, a true Godsend. So why did this revelation bother her so much?

Because she wanted to be more to him than a proving ground or a mission. She wanted much more. She wanted life to be bigger and brighter, as it always was when Brett was around. She wanted his companionship, his love…marriage.

Brett grasped her hands and pulled her close. "It doesn't matter what happened in the past or what brought me here. My feelings for you are real, Rafaela. I hope you believe that."

She searched his eyes, looking for the truth. She couldn't find what she wanted. But it didn't seem to matter as he pulled her into his arms and kissed her. *I do believe you, Brett. I do. And heaven help us both if that's a mistake.*

~*~

Rafaela's cellphone chirped. She paused from proof-reading the invitations. Laurie's name flashed across the screen. "That cinches it. I'm sure Laurie's got a contact at the newspaper who's feeding her information."

Brett was rifling through his ever-present box of tools to finish some work on a display. "How can you be so sure?"

"Because she's been calling non-stop ever since my meeting with the advertising rep this morning."

"She wants to know what you'll be putting in the series of ads you just purchased."

"Yep."

"I guess it's a good thing you didn't tell them. Your demand for secrecy might just buy us a little more time to get our program in place."

"It's a little disturbing to discover how desperate Angie is to know what's going on. This is the third vendor she's approached."

Brett rose and shrugged. "There's a way to stop it, or at least prevent more info drain."

"How?"

"You've just invested a substantial amount of money in advertising with the newspaper. Call and tell them your privacy has been violated and you're canceling the ads."

"Wow. You do play hardball, don't you?"

Brett shrugged again. "Word will spread like wildfire amongst your vendors and your event will become the best-kept secret in Santa Fe."

"Still, the newspaper is our best venue for cultural events. I'm not sure we can afford to pull our ads."

"For the price we're paying, we can buy a lot of posters and plaster them all over town, not to mention how much mileage we'll get out of our social media. But I think you'll find that won't be necessary. The newspaper doesn't want to lose your business. They may even offer you a better deal."

She hesitated.

"Would you like me to do it for you?"

"No." Her response was quick.

Brett's smile was just as immediate. He touched a fingertip to her nose before bending back down. "I didn't think so."

She gave him a playful nudge. "Go. Build while I stretch out of my comfort zone." Actually, she'd been doing a lot of stretching in the weeks since they'd finalized the contract with the Madrigals.

Brett insisted that the opening be by invitation only. He felt it would build anticipation for the event.

Together, she and Brett had sketched primitive ideas for posters, written press releases, and purchased radio and print ads. Their updated website was just waiting to go live.

The gallery's back storeroom was now a showroom, thanks to Brett's deft carpentry. Knee-high walls created a maze-like path from piece to piece but still left open space for viewing all the pieces at once. Rafaela would choose the paint colors after the Madrigals visited next week.

They were personally delivering their work, driving from Sedona to Santa Fe with their daughter, Christie. Troy had expressed an interest in the architecture of the rancho, and Lucia had offered their home as a place to stay.

The Madrigals's work had inspired Rafaela. She'd seen pictures, and her imagination had soared. She had ideas of how to stage the artwork, but she couldn't wait to meet Troy and Eliza personally and add their input to her concepts. She'd discovered she loved this business of collaboration, especially with Brett.

Rafaela's excitement outweighed any nervousness

she might have had about meeting people Brett considered his family. He spoke of them so fondly, she'd come to think of them as friends rather than stars of the art world.

Her mother was in a happy tizzy of cleaning and cooking for their guests. Sofia was Rafaela's only concern. She'd feared her sister would slip into one of her patterns of binging and purging. But so far, Sofia had handled the furor by immersing herself in her painting but was also taking regular, healthy breaks.

Life was good. It would be better as soon as this phone call was over. She bounced her pencil eraser against her desk, waiting for the ad rep to pick up her phone.

"Hello."

Rafaela took a deep breath and plunged right in. "Alicia, this is Rafaela de Silva. I'm afraid we have a problem, and I'll be pulling my ads." She explained her reasons and her certainty that someone at the paper had shared her information. "I specifically told you I wanted this kept quiet until its release."

Alicia apologized profusely but didn't even try to deny it. Obviously she knew, or at least suspected, who was responsible for the breach of confidence. "I assure you, my editor will be made fully aware of this unprofessional conduct, and he'll deal with it personally. In the meantime, I hope you'll reconsider pulling the ads. Surely we can find some way to make it up to you."

Rafaela smiled. Brett was right...again. That happened with such regularity that it might become annoying—when her business wasn't benefitting so much from his advice. She agreed to a double run of ads at no additional cost and headed back to share the news with Brett. "You were right."

Brett lay flat on the ground trying to "eyeball" a measurement. "Let me guess. Double the ads."

She crouched down beside him. "Yes. Should I bow and kiss your hand in proper respect for the king of public relations?"

"No bowing, but I'll take a kiss." Moving quickly, he wrapped a hand around her neck and pulled her down.

She squealed as she tumbled, sprawling on top of him in a flurry of long skirts, flying hair and laughter.

In another swift movement, he rolled over and scooped her beneath him. The laughter died on her lips as he kissed her long and deep. The touch of his firm, soft lips ignited her senses. Each time he touched her, yearning built inside, and it threatened to overwhelm her.

All doubts fled. Rafaela knew with certainty that she'd fallen in love with Brett Fraser. She loved teasing him, working side-by-side, and laughing at his jokes. She adored how he cared for her sister and mother, how he looked at the world with smiling eyes, and how, when she stumbled and fell, he picked her up with one glance from those flashing hazel eyes. Everything about him made her heart sing. The need to love him in all ways grew like a fire every time he touched her.

Her heart quailed. Would that fire consume her? She loved and feared God and dreaded losing her self-control and commitment to His rules. But most of all, what she didn't see in Brett's eyes gave her pause. The love and passion she felt for him was missing from his gaze.

She didn't doubt he was attracted to her, or that he

cared about her. But his touch, while tender and gentle, held none of the heat she felt and longed to see returned. His actions made it clear he valued her as a person, but a veil drifted between them. Wispy and filmy, it hid a secret, some truth Brett dared not reveal. And until she knew what that was, she couldn't give her heart completely.

She pushed against his chest. "I need to get those invitation proofs back to the printer."

He rolled away without a backward glance. "And I need to finish this measurement. Why don't you pick up some lunch on your way back?"

Rafaela rose to her feet and smoothed her skirt with fingers that trembled. She glanced at Brett's steady hands. Stifling a sigh, she flipped her hair over her shoulder and headed out the door.

Mid-summer in Santa Fe and monsoon season was upon them. During the rainy season, fluffy clouds would build along the distant mountain ridges. By afternoon, those clouds turned black and then, with little warning, opened up and dumped watery contents in a deluge. Streets flooded with the downpour and washed everything clean. Then the skies cleared and rainbows danced across.

Rafaela loved monsoon season, the sudden downpours, the green hills, and the tourists spilling into the plaza. Almost daily, a band would play on the grassy common. Natives of Santa Fe pulled up lawn chairs and picnic baskets. Strangers slowed down to mingle and share a story or two.

Since the first days of its settlement on the Turquoise Trail, Santa Fe had been a crossroads of cultures, a meeting and resting place for travelers from all over the world. Things had not changed. Buildings fell and were rebuilt, but the essence, the soul of Santa Fe, stayed the same.

She hurried across the busy street, hoping to catch the printer before he left for lunch. The only requirement Rafaela had made for the showing was that they use local businesses. Brett completely agreed, even when the cost might have been lower if they'd used larger, nationally known corporations.

To keep the invitation information private, she'd dealt exclusively with the owner. Mr. Winchell left for lunch promptly at one every day. With an eye to the dark clouds above, Rafaela picked up her pace and ran across the grass, the full, ruffled hem of her long skirt fanning out ahead of her with each step.

She caught Mr. Winchell in time. They discussed the details for the final printing, and Rafaela headed back outside. The clouds had grown darker. She hoped to order their food and make it back to the shop before the downfall.

She hurried along the sidewalk, headed for her favorite restaurant. Ducking her head as the first raindrops began to fall, she scooted inside and came to a sudden halt.

At a table tucked into an intimate corner, Emilio sat across from Rafaela's chief competitor—her former friend, Angie.

11

Emilio looked up and gave her a casual wave and smile.

Rafaela's pulse skipped and then stuttered back into a steady beat. Swallowing hard, she returned the wave and then moved to the counter to place her to-go order. Her glance continued to stray back to the table.

She hadn't seen Angie in a while. Her old friend looked as if she'd lost weight. Her slender form was almost too thin, but every bobbed blonde hair on her head was in place and done in the latest style. She wore a pencil-straight blue dress with short sleeves and a dark blue belt buckled to her impossibly narrow waist.

Always the epitome of fashion. Angie managed to make Rafaela feel slightly insecure. Still, she looked as if she belonged on a busy New York sidewalk, not here on Santa Fe's plaza.

Rafaela's own peasant-style top and slightly ruffled skirt fit the feel and flair of her hometown. She knew who she was and where she belonged, and that knowledge lent her a comforting confidence. Rafaela flipped her long dark hair over her shoulder, grasped her to-go bag, and headed for the door.

"Rafaela, wait. I need to talk to you."

She glanced back.

Emilio had risen from his seat. He said something quiet to Angie then grasped her hand in an intimate way.

As he walked toward Rafaela, Angie turned and shot her a look so virulent, so full of animosity and hatred that Rafaela gasped.

"What is it?" Emilio touched her arm and looked back.

Angie turned away, leaving visible only the perfectly coiffed back of her perfectly shaped head.

"Are you OK?" Emilio asked.

Doubting what she'd seen, Rafaela spun and walked quickly to the door.

The sprinkle of rain suddenly released a deluge. She and Emilio were forced to back up against the building as the rain splattered and splashed the sidewalk. The damp, musty smell of wet asphalt soon gave way to a fresh, clean scent of rainfall. Something about that pleasant, unsoiled fragrance washed away the disturbing feelings Angie had ignited.

Rafaela had been mistaken. Surely Angie could not possibly harbor such animosity toward her. They'd had their differences but they'd once been friends. She was overreacting, possibly because of Emilio's presence.

"You're not going to get crazy about my meeting Angie, are you?"

Rafaela looked up at her tall friend. Hard to believe this six-foot giant was the boy she used to beat in races and climbing trees. A deep crease cut into his handsome forehead.

She smiled. "Do I have a reason to get crazy?"

"Of course not. Angie and I...well, it's personal."

He meant to reassure her. Instead, a ripple of fear shivered its way through her carefully maintained control.

"You didn't mention the showing, did you?"

"I'm not stupid, Rafaela. I know how things stand between you two. But—well, we have some history...some unresolved past."

The two had dated briefly in high school, but Angie's parents had disapproved. The relationship ended badly. It was something Emilio never discussed.

"And you decided to resolve those issues right now, just before the most important event of your career, knowing how she feels about my gallery?"

"It just sort of happened. We bumped into each other and things grew from there."

Another coincidence. Brett's concerns drifted through her mind like a shadow. Was he right? How could so many things line up against her? The sheer number of oddities didn't seem normal or natural. Or maybe some of Brett's issues were creeping into her psyche. Part of the reason he was on sabbatical was to forget his past. She wanted to help him overcome his bad memories and anxieties, to ease them, not to succumb to them herself.

But that near-murderous glare Angie had cast her way...If Rafaela hadn't misinterpreted that chilling glare, the woman definitely disliked her enough to cause her harm. A deep shudder wracked her frame.

"You're cold. The rain's let up. Let's get you inside."

Emilio took her arm and hurried across the street. They ducked and leaped across the rain-swollen gutter. Once they were safe under the portico of the gallery building, Emilio gave her arm a squeeze. "Gotta run. I'm helping Mom with the birthday celebrations for Grandfather. You're still planning on coming aren't you?"

"Of course." Emilio's grandfather was celebrating his ninetieth birthday. Paul Hastings had been one of Rafaela's grandfather's life-long trio of companions. Paul's family owned the land adjacent to the de Silva rancho. Between their two properties ran a spit of land belonging to a Pueblo tribe and their friend Ruben Lucero.

The three men had grown up together, roaming the countryside between Santa Fe and Taos. They uncovered the Chaco artifacts after Ruben's father determined that the mound was not a burial ground.

Eventually, Ruben became a tribal leader and Paul married Ruben's sister. All three of the families stayed close over the years. In fact, Emilio was more like a cousin than a friend, and that thought gave Rafaela pause.

He squeezed her arm in a goodbye and she grasped it, a sense of trepidation filling her entire being. "Wait. I don't want to pry, Emilio, but promise me you'll be careful. Promise me you won't let Angie use you to get back at me."

Her friend held her hand tight. With his black hair falling over his forehead, he looked like the young boy he'd once been. The sight tugged at her heart.

"I promise. I have my reasons for what I'm doing, and they don't include getting seriously involved with Angie. I know better than that." He squeezed her hand one last time, and then leapt back across the rain-filled gutter.

~*~

"Oh my goodness, you're beautiful!"
Brett chuckled. "Leave it to you to get right to the

point."

The Madrigals had just pulled into the horseshoe drive of the ranch. Troy, Eliza, and Christie had barely stepped out of the car when Eliza made her bold statement.

"Well, she is." Eliza grasped both Rafaela's hands and faced her. "You should have introduced us sooner, Brett. I can't wait to get to know her." She lifted Rafaela's clasped hands and met her gaze. "It's easy to see how you caught his eye, but what I really want to know is how you captured his heart."

Rafaela shot Brett a shy, embarrassed look. "I'm not sure I really have."

Her questioning gaze gave Brett a momentary pause. But not for long. The amazing picture the two women made together entranced him. Both petite, they stood almost at the same height. Two lovely women in complete contrast. Eliza with her wild, curling mane of red hair and delicate, pale features. Rafaela's long, silky black tresses, bold red lips and dark eyes. They created a perfect picture.

"Boy, I wish I could paint body shapes. Look at them." Sofia murmured beside him.

Glad he wasn't the only one struck by the image, he pulled out his phone and handed it to her. "Quick. Snap a picture before they move and save it for later. You *will* learn how to paint them." Brett stepped across to Troy and they shook hands with much back patting. "I see Eliza hasn't changed much."

His tall, distinguished friend shook his head. "Would you have it any other way?"

"No." He released Troy and pulled Eliza toward him. "I hate to break you two up, but I need a hug too." He grasped her in a deep embrace. "I've missed you."

When they pulled away, Eliza's eyes swam in a pool of tears. She gave him a playful tap. "Don't stay away so long next time."

Christie stood behind her mother.

Brett held out his arms to the thirteen-year-old and she came to him quickly. "I think you've grown an inch since I last saw you. You look great."

Meaning she looked healthy. Christie suffered from rheumatoid arthritis and, for a time, had depended on a wheelchair to get around. Now she stood tall and straight.

"What have you been doing?"

"I'm riding again. Mom and Dad bought me a horse."

"I might have known a horse brought that sparkle to your eyes. I'm just glad it wasn't a boy."

She blushed and quickly let the sleeves of her loose-knit top slip over her hands, but not before Brett caught a glimpse of them. They were beginning to swan, the telltale misshaping that defined sufferers of R.A. Even with this slight disfigurement, Christie appeared healthy and happy.

Maybe she could share her insights with Sofia.

Two years Christie's senior, Sofia should have been more confident and comfortable. Instead, she clung to her mother's arm, almost hiding behind Lucia's slender form.

Brett had to take the teen's hand and drag her out to introduce her.

Christie's warm smile was met by a mumbled greeting and a duck of the head.

But Brett wasn't giving up. He knew the girls had a great deal in common, and he was counting on

Christie's outgoing personality to draw Sofia out.

"Let me show you to your rooms so you can get comfortable." Rafaela led the way into the house.

Brett stayed behind to help Troy with their bags. They loaded the crate-packed artwork into Brett's studio, and then hefted suitcases into the back rooms of the U-shaped house.

Brett carried Christie's bags into Sofia's room and found Christie alone, looking very uncomfortable. "Where do you want this?"

She hesitated before gesturing to a corner.

"You're OK with sharing a room with Sofia, aren't you?"

"It's fine with me, but I don't think she wants me in here. She took off as soon as she could."

Brett frowned. "It's not you. Sofia is painfully shy. I think she's afraid people will say something about how she looks."

Christie perked up. "Yeah, she's pretty thin."

"She has an eating disorder and she's really self-conscious about her appearance."

The young girl raised her eyebrows. "Boy, do I get that."

"I know you do. But you're doing so well, I thought you might be able to point Sofia in the right direction."

She shrugged. "It'll be kinda hard if she avoids me the whole time I'm here."

"Don't worry." Brett gestured for her to follow him. "I know all her hiding places and exactly how to get her to talk."

Christie followed him out the door and straight to Sofia's favorite painting spot. Even though he'd repaired the fence, the shade beneath the Palo Verde tree was still Sofia's go-to-spot when she was deep into a painting.

Sure enough, the teen was positioned with her back to the house, facing the distant mountains. A picture of the once-tilted front gates filled the canvas and was almost complete. The stunning turquoise of the gates was eye-catching.

Christie gasped even before they stopped. "Wow. That's awesome. I wish I could hold a brush long enough to do something like that."

Christie's statement caught Sofia off guard, and she turned with a puzzled expression on her face. "What do you mean? Anyone can hold a brush."

"Not me." Christie pulled her sleeves back for Sofia to get a good view of her slightly elongated fingers.

"Hey, your hands look like the ones in my paintings. I can never get them to look quite right..." Suddenly realizing she'd just insulted Christie, she trailed off and her face flushed.

Brett chuckled. "Maybe you should be painting pictures of people with Christie's disease."

"You have a disease?" Sofia's eyes were large, dark pools, overtaking her face.

Christy nodded. "Rheumatoid arthritis. It's painful and crippling. Someday all my joints will look like this."

"But you're so beautiful, like your mother. You have her gorgeous red hair, and your skin...it glows."

Now it was Christie's turn to blush. "I'm not beautiful. I'm all elbows and knees and braces."

Sofia tilted her head. "I'd love to paint you."

Christie laughed and turned to Brett. "Is she serious?"

Brett touched her shoulder. "She's a very good artist, Christie. She knows what she's saying."

Sofia straightened a little after his comment. "Do you have a purple top?"

"No." Christie laughed. "That's way too bright for me."

Sofia shook her head. "Trust me; you're going to be amazed at what it will do for your skin. I think my mother has a shawl we can use. We'll ask. Just let me clean up these brushes."

Brett slipped away, smiling. His presence was no longer needed. He grinned all the way back to the house.

Just before he reached the French doors, his cellphone buzzed. He recognized the number of Rafaela's mechanic on the screen and punched it to answer. "Joe, I didn't know you worked on Saturdays."

"Normally I don't. But I felt bad about having Rafaela's truck for so long. I decided to work on it on my own time."

"Well, thanks. I know she'll appreciate it but we've been getting along OK. Hope it didn't make too much trouble for you."

"Honestly, Brett. That's part of it. I couldn't put my finger on the problem. I kept looking for these difficult repairs. In the end, it was a simple fix but created another issue. That's why I called you."

"What do you mean?"

"Someone put diesel fuel in Rafaela's unleaded engine. I drained the fuel and replaced the filters. Like I said, an easy fix, but it concerns me that someone purposely dumped the wrong fuel in her car."

A prickly sensation started at the back of Brett's

neck. "What makes you think it was on purpose? Maybe Rafaela picked up the wrong pump when she gassed up."

"No way. A diesel nozzle doesn't fit in an unleaded tank. And even if it did, once you run diesel fuel through an engine designed for unleaded gas, the impact is immediate. The engine shuts down. That truck sits at the back of her shop every day, all day. Everyone knows that. I'm telling you, someone dumped diesel into her tank just to cause mischief. It could have been kids, but why would they waste money on diesel fuel for a prank?"

Brett didn't have an answer.

"It wasn't Rafaela's mistake or kids." Joe's emphatic tone increased Brett's steadily growing anxiety. "Someone's trying to cause trouble for Rafaela and I'm so sure of it, I bought her a locking cap to replace her old one."

12

"I'm sorry Tío Aaron won't be here for dinner again." Rafaela stood beside her mother in the kitchen, helping assemble Lucia's famous chicken enchiladas. Grandfather Hastings had specifically asked Lucia to bring the dish to his birthday celebration tomorrow. They were preparing a triple batch to serve for dinner tonight.

Her mother shrugged. "It's all right. I'm actually a little relieved. Aaron doesn't approve of Brett or his friends. I think the Madrigals are perfectly delightful, and I'm having a wonderful time. I'm almost glad Aaron's not here to spoil it."

Rafaela paused and held her red enchilada-sauce-covered hands in the air. "I don't understand. Well, I understand why Tío still doesn't trust Brett, but what does he have against the Madrigals? He knows their reputation. Surely he can't believe they have some diabolical plot to take advantage of us. Why is he being so difficult?"

Her mother sighed. "I don't know. I never realized how much Aaron is like your father. Both of them hate change. Frankly, I'm very disappointed in Aaron. I thought he understood how difficult Rafael's attitudes made my life. And I *know* he knows how determined I am to change."

Rafaela bit her lower lip. Her mother had never spoken about her relationship with Tío Aaron. And

Rafaela could not remember a time her mother had expressed resentment toward her father and his slavish devotion to his painting.

She didn't want to spoil or slow down the revelations with a startled response. Silently, she took the rolled tortilla, placed it in the casserole dish and waited for her mother to continue.

"I know Aaron's never been close to Sofia, not like he is with you. But still, you'd think he'd be happy for my sake, if not for hers."

"Wait, happy about what?" Too startled to hold back her response, Rafaela turned to her mother.

"Troy wants to enroll Sofia in the Fallon School of Art."

"When did he say this?"

"Last night when you and Brett ran to the grocery store for me."

Rafaela almost put her sauce-covered hands on her hips before she caught herself. "And you just now decided to discuss this with me."

Her mother leveled a look on Rafaela that made her feel ten years old. "There's nothing to discuss. I know you feel responsible, but I'm her mother, and I've already decided. If they offer her a scholarship, we'll go. Sofia's beside herself with excitement."

"Of course she is, until it's time to leave. Then she'll eat herself into a frenzy or stop eating completely."

"Yes, that's probably true. But if she stumbles, I'll pick her up, dust her off, and send her on her way again."

Rafaela shook her head. "Why? Why would you even put her through that?"

"Because there's a chance she might make it,

Rafaela, and I have to give her that chance. Don't you see? It's a gift from God. A month or two ago, would you have ever imagined this opportunity would come her way?"

"Not even in my wildest dreams."

"Exactly. It's a God-given chance. If He sent it our way then He must have a plan for her."

Rafaela shook her head. "She doesn't have the strength for this."

Her mother inhaled deeply. "Then we will rely on His strength. She will make it. I have faith."

Sofia and Christie's chatter echoed down the hall as they walked toward the kitchen. Rafaela and her mother quickly turned back to the enchiladas.

Rafaela sighed. She didn't have quite as much faith as her mother, and if this didn't work out, she'd be the one picking up the pieces.

The Madrigals showing had to get the gallery back on its feet. It absolutely had to be a success. She would need the money to take care of her sister.

~*~

The Hastings's ranch rested in the rolling hills just outside of Santa Fe. Although not as old as the de Silva's rancho, the property had belonged to the Hastings family for many generations. Paul Hastings was the patriarch of a large and sprawling family of mixed ethnic backgrounds—Anglo, Pueblo, and Spanish.

To Brett's pleasure, Grandfather Hastings's birthday celebration offered a sampling of all three cultures.

Tables had been set out beneath a copious grove of

cottonwood trees. A barbecue pit churned out steaks from Hastings cattle and chickens. A goat roasted in a deep pit, and several tables sagged with the weight of salsas, beans, chili dishes, fresh garden vegetables, and of, course, baskets of Brett's new personal favorite—homemade sopaipillas.

The family gathered early to sing and wish Grandfather a happy birthday. Groups took turns greeting the ninety-year-old. Brett and Rafaela's group was at the end of a long line of well-wishers when Lucia glanced around.

"Aaron should be here. He said he'd be late, but I didn't think this late."

"He'll be here, Mama."

"I'm not so sure. He and Paul have had their differences over the years, but Aaron said he wanted to be here, especially to meet the Madrigals."

"He's just running late. He's been so busy lately." Rafaela pointed out the movement of the line.

Distracted, Lucia turned to greet the birthday honoree. Even though the line of greeters had been long, when Lucia introduced Brett and the Madrigals, the elderly gentleman's gaze grew bright and sharp.

Brett shook his hand and Mr. Hastings held the grip a tad longer.

"So you are the young man courting our little Rafaela."

Brett grinned and glanced back at a blushing Rafaela. "Well, I'm not sure she'll call it that but, yes, I guess I am."

The old man nodded. "Stay a while. I want to talk to you." He gestured to a nearby chair.

Brett looked at Rafaela who gave him a puzzled shrug. Brett waited as a few more family members paid their respects. Occasionally, the old man would glance Brett's way, as if studying him, maybe judging his character. Brett should have felt uncomfortable, but there was something reassuring and solid about Paul Hastings. Something that made Brett curious to hear what the man had to say.

At last, the line eased and Mr. Hastings turned. Gripping his cane, he faced Brett. "My grandson, Emilio, tells me you are very important in the world of art."

Brett shook his head. "I'm not important at all. But I do know people who are."

Mr. Hasting's narrowed his eyes. Once blue, they were gray now with film. Still, Brett felt as if the rheumy gaze pierced straight through him.

"My grandson says your event will do great things for him and our little Rafaela."

Brett grinned again. "I'll bet she hates it when you call her 'little Rafaela.'"

A ghost of a smile whispered across the older man's lips. "You know her well. Do you doubt my right to call her that?"

"Not you. But there might be others I'd question."

Paul Hastings's gaze settled on something in the distance.

Brett turned.

Aaron Pomeroy had pulled up in his sedan and stepped out of his car.

Lucia waved across the grassy expanse and crossed toward him.

Hastings nodded very slowly. "You might be just what our little girl needs."

Was he warning Brett or simply letting his mind wander as a man his age might? Brett wasn't sure, and

Hastings fell silent. For a long while, it seemed he was lost in his own thoughts. Then he said, "Emilio says you are from New York. Will you take Rafaela away?"

Brett looked around at the family gathered beneath the ancient shade trees, the beautiful blue sky and shook his head. "Why would I want to take her away from this?"

Another wispy smile floated over Hastings's lips and he nodded. "Good. She belongs here. This land is in her blood, like her grandfather before her."

Brett hesitated. "She told me you and her grandfather were great friends and that you helped him uncover the Chaco artifacts that gave him his start in business."

"Yes. We were young and foolish. We didn't know what we were doing then. Fortunately, Ruben's father was there and determined the mound was a rubbish pile. Still, he offered prayers and burned sage." Paul Hastings's voice dipped low and he nodded as if affirming a statement to ghostly listeners. The air seemed charged with electricity and Brett leaned closer, straining to hear the older man's words.

The laughter of playing children broke out nearby and echoed like something far away, maybe with the voices of a people long gone.

"Ruben's father told us that if the mound was a refuse dump, then somewhere nearby would be the village. But we never looked."

Brett's heart pounded. It made sense. Only a village could create a refuse mound. A whole village. Uncovered. Somewhere on Rafaela's land. Could this be what the I.C.E. was desperately trying to locate, the secret cache of Native American artifacts being looted and sold on the black market?

If it were true, then a valuable archaeological site was being destroyed. A site that could be worth a small fortune to Rafaela and her family. All her financial problems would be resolved...if Brett could find the location.

Brett's thoughts came to a skittering halt. He was certain Mr. Hastings knew more than he was admitting. He'd wanted to speak to Brett to see what kind of man he was, to know where he stood and maybe to warn him.

"Why didn't you all search for the village, Mr. Hastings? Mr. de Silva used the money to start his business. What stopped you from searching for more?"

A now-familiar, wispy smile floated over the man's lips. "Something happened." The old man shook his head. "In the 1930's, a health spa opened at the mineral hot springs on the mountain. My father had a bad back. He often went to the spa for treatment and one time he took my friends and me." He gripped his cane with both hands, and his gray eyes gazed into the distance. "As my father finished his treatment, we slipped outside to wait. We found a natural spring behind the building and followed it into the hills. There was an old cemetery. It covered maybe half an acre and the headstones all bore the names of Native Americans. Ruben, Gabriel, and I couldn't believe our eyes. All the graves had been dug up.

"We walked that entire cemetery, we three boys, and every...single...grave had been dug up by pothunters. They even tore up the graves of the little ones."

The old man shook his head. "We left that day and swore never to uncover a mound again. Not ever." Mr. Hastings turned to Brett. "Not one of us broke that vow. Not even when times were hard and we needed the money." His look and his tone implied that he wouldn't break that vow even now. Not for any reason.

Brett nodded. "I understand, sir."

Paul Hasting studied him for a moment and then nodded. "I think you do, young man. I think you really do."

Rafaela bent her knees to her chest, smoothed her long skirt over her legs, and wrapped her arms around them.

Brett had stretched on the blanket beside her without a word.

She was dying to know what Grandfather Hastings had discussed, but Brett hadn't opened up. Maybe now would be her chance to ask.

He placed his hands behind his head and looked up at a sky turning from mauve to pink as the sun sank behind the mountains. "It looks like the afternoon rain passed us by today."

"Don't hold your breath. Those clouds can roll in faster than you realize."

"Everything is moving faster than me right now. I ate too much."

Rafaela laughed and closed her eyes too. This day couldn't have been more perfect. The food had been wonderful.

Emilio and the Madrigals had spent most of the afternoon talking. Then Emilio had taken them around, introducing them to other artists. Several of Emilio's family members worked in silver and some worked with pottery. Troy and Eliza had barely sat all afternoon, they were so wrapped up in the conversations.

Rafaela opened her eyes to look for her mother, who was saying goodbye to Tío Aaron near his car. After greeting Grandfather, Tío had paid his respects to several other family members.

Lucia had introduced him to the Madrigals, but he'd purposely avoided Brett.

Right from the beginning, those two had butted heads. Tío Aaron had treated Brett badly. Her mother said Tío thought Brett was trying to worm his way into their lives to take advantage of them.

Rafaela understood her adopted uncle's concerns. She'd had them herself in the beginning. Her mother tried to explain to Tío how helpful Brett had been, but that hadn't changed her uncle's opinion. He and her mother had exchanged heated words over his stay in the studio. Rafaela couldn't remember a time when her mother and Tío had fought.

Apparently, it happened again because her mother spun abruptly and stalked back to the tables. Her frowning expression confirmed Rafaela's suspicions, and she sighed. The last thing she wanted was for her uncle's stubborn attitude to spoil what had been a wonderful day. Putting the thought behind her, she looked away.

Beneath the shade of a large cottonwood, a small stage had been erected with a wooden dance floor in front. Musicians set up their instruments and tuned guitars.

Emilio's uncles stacked hunks of wood in a fire pit and coated the wood with a starter. As the flames shot up, a group of nearby teenage girls squealed and danced away.

Sofia and Christie were amongst them.

"I don't know what you did, but those two are becoming fast friends."

Brett opened his eyes.

Rafaela gestured to Christie and Sofia, surrounded by the group of young Hastings cousins.

"Simple. I started talking about painting. Christie's been around art all of her life. She knew enough to be interested and voilà, a friendship was formed."

She turned to him. "How do you do that?"

"What? Bring two teenagers with common interests together? That's easy." He rolled over onto his stomach, propped an elbow, and leaned his head on his hand. "The really tough thing was getting a certain lovely lady to open up to me."

Frowning, she fluffed the hem of her skirt. "Maybe that's because a certain lady has a hard time believing in 'happily-ever-after.'"

Sighing, Brett rose to a sitting position. "I don't know how that's even possible when you're surrounded by this." He gestured to the family, to the children playing and couples laughing and loving.

She shook her head. "Maybe *this* was the reason. I grew up with this big extended family. We all got along and loved each other. I thought the whole world was a 'happily-ever-after' until my father died. Then I learned that things are not always what they seem."

He placed a hand behind her and leaned close, so close his breath tickled her shoulder. "Is that why you still don't trust me?"

She turned her head and their lips were a breath away. "The truth is very important to me, Brett. Earlier, you told Grandfather you were courting me. That's something serious to him. Did you mean it?"

"Every word."

She searched for the truth in his eyes and found it. Perhaps shadows still flitted around the edges but, for the first time, no doubts held her back. Leaning forward, she kissed him.

"Rafaela!"

She broke the kiss with great reluctance.

Her mother stood in the center of the dance floor and gestured to the musicians. "They want us to dance."

The guitar players were already running riffs on their guitars.

Rafaela shook her head. "Not right now. Go ahead."

Her mother smiled, waved, and clapped in time with the music.

"You and your mother dance?"

She nodded. "Flamenco."

"Flamenco?" His surprised tone gave her pause. "Then you must know Alexander Summers's work."

"Yes, of course. But he plays modern stuff. We're more traditionalists. My mother traveled the country and even performed in Europe."

She shrugged. "There were dancers in my father's family, too. In fact, one family tradition says one of ancestors was such a famous dancer that she was kidnapped by a nobleman and brought here with the conquistadors. Her true love sold everything, even his guitar to follow her. They were reunited here in the new world and started a family. My father used to tease my mother that the only reason he introduced himself was because she bore his famous ancestor's name."

"Lucia. Their names were Juan and Lucia."

The shocked expression on Brett's face startled her.

"How do you know that?"

"I've heard this legend before."

"How? From whom?"

"Alex Summers. He owns La Guitarra, Juan's instrument. Alex tells the story of parted lovers every time he performs. He's going to flip when I tell him his lovers found each other."

Rafaela's lips parted in surprise. "My family's tale is true? Juan and Lucia were real?"

"Real enough to spawn their own legend. But that's not what's important to us, Rafaela." He grasped her arms and turned her toward him. "Of all the places I could have gone, of all the people I could have run across, I met you. I know you've doubted me...doubted us. But you can't possibly doubt this. God brought us together. This, *we* are God's plan." His eyes sparkled with a delightful inner light. The clasp of his hands was strong and secure.

Everything she'd ever wanted seemed within her reach, except passion.

His touch and his gaze still lacked that electric emotion.

She needed—deserved—his passion.

"Rafaela, come!"

Her mother's voice distracted her again. She turned to see Emilio's cousins laughing and charging up the hill toward them.

"Sorry, man," Eduardo, the youngest Hastings said to Brett. "It's just not a party unless Rafaela dances."

Shouting, they lifted her off the blanket by her

arms and carried her away. She looked back over her shoulder.

Smiling, Brett rose and followed them down the hill.

Her mother held out her dance shoes. Rafaela shook her head. "Did you plan this?"

Mama laughed. "Brett deserves to know what he's getting into."

A chair magically appeared behind Rafaela. Shaking her head, she sat and buckled her shoes.

Her mother grasped her hands and spun around her with a flourish of skirts.

Rafaela smiled and closed her eyes, listening to the music.

Her mother edged up behind her.

Yes, Brett deserved to know. This was how she and her mother faced life and survived, back to back. Hands clasped. United.

Rafaela tested her ankle. It felt strong. She tilted her head back, touching her mother's, ready.

The guitars began a beat and a singer cried out, his voice echoing the mournful cry of their people.

She and her mother lifted their arms in unison, raising, rounding gracefully and falling. Right. Then left.

The beat of the guitarist's hand on the wooden instrument called to Rafaela. Stamp with her pointed toe. Then tap for the heel to come down hard. Again with the right. Stamp and tap. Her mother's clicking heels matched hers.

Stamp and tap. *Plante y golpa*. The words flowed through her mind and her body obeyed.

Plante y golpa. Stomp and tap. Faster and faster, until their tapping matched the pounding beat of the guitars. Rounded arms. Wrists spinning in graceful twirls. Faster and faster until Mama made the *llamada*, the call to the guitarists to slow the pace.

Rafaela grasped her skirt and spun. Now they faced each other. *Plante. Golpa.* Dark skirts swishing from side to side. Moving closer then brushing around each other. Coming back together again.

She loved dancing with her mother in perfect harmony. Both their movements synchronized. Their blood answering the beat and the rhythm of their ancestors.

Her mother made the call again. *Plante. Golpa.* Stamp. Tap. Faster and faster. Rafaela's feet tapped harder and harder. Her hair flowed like a black veil against her face, from side to side. Faster and faster.

This time her mother didn't make the *llamada*. This time she began to clap her hands in the *jaleo*, the talk.

"*Ole.*"

She spun around, facing Rafaela, challenging her.

"*Eso es! Ole!*" She called, clapping faster.

Rafaela laughed with pure pleasure and tapped. Grabbing her skirt, she spun around.

Her gaze landed on Brett. He leaned against a tree, his fingertips tucked into his jeans. His eyes burned with all the heat and passion she'd been waiting to see.

His look lit a fire in Rafaela. With the music of her ancestors flowing through her veins, she began the tap again, hips moving as she swayed. Faster and faster. Rafaela wove her arms up, lifted her hair and let it cascade down her back. Her feet matched the pace of the furious guitars, strumming and pounding. She looked up at a dark sky full of stars and watched the smoke streaming to heaven. Flaming embers floated up on the heated air, like her prayers. She'd waited so long for a moment like this...for this man. He was everything she'd ever wanted.

"Gracias, Dios. Gracias," she whispered.

Then she made the *llamada*, signaling the ending to the musicians. Lifting her arms in a dramatic gesture, she spun and dropped to the ground just as the guitars strummed the last riff. With her head bowed, Rafaela waited for the clapping. But none came. Lifting her gaze, she saw that Brett had crossed the wooden dance floor and now stood above her, his hands outstretched.

Breathing heavily, she took them. He pulled her up. But when she thought he would release her, he clasped her around the waist and spun her so fast her hair flew around them. Bending her back over his arm, he kissed her long and hard—right in front of the whole gathering.

The audience burst into applause and cheers.

Her mother's voice rang out the loudest. *"Ole!"*

13

"Are you sure?"

Rafaela sat on the floor of the gallery, a large paintbrush in her hands. She made a fetching picture with mauve paint smeared on her jeans and speckled across her cheeks. If the topic of the conversation hadn't been of such a serious nature, he would have sat beside her and kissed her.

"Joe was absolutely positive. That's why he bought you a locking gas cap."

They were just one day away from the showing, and Brett had finally found the time to tell her about his conversation with the mechanic.

They'd been so busy. Everyone had pitched in. Eliza and the girls even volunteered to give the gallery a good cleaning, and they'd organized the canvases in the small room behind the desk. The group had called a halt to the work early today, leaving Brett and Rafaela alone to finish some details.

He squatted beside her. "Do you believe me now?"

She nodded. "I have to. It's pretty hard to ignore the truth. But I almost wished you hadn't told me. Now I'll worry."

He had more to tell her, more truths he'd kept back, but one revelation at a time was enough. "I almost didn't tell you because I knew you'd worry. But I discussed it with Troy and together we've been taking some extra precautions, as quietly as possible. We don't want your mother or Eliza and the girls to be concerned."

"Good idea. You don't know how disconcerting it is to realize someone is trying to hurt you."

He smiled. "Actually, I've been in your position."

"Oh, that's right. I forgot." Her smile was slight. "I still can't understand who—" She stopped abruptly.

"What is it?"

"The day I ordered the invitations, I saw Emilio with Angie. When his back was turned, she looked at me with such, well, hatred, I think. There was something venomous in her expression, and it really shook me. I don't think I've ever seen so much virulence on a face."

"Emilio's coming in later. I'll talk to him and see if he knows anything."

"I'm sure it's Angie. Once we confront her, all this nonsense will stop."

Brett didn't remind her that Angie had never been close enough to her running shoes to slice the lace. Someone else—someone close to Rafaela—had to be the source of her problems. He wanted to keep that thought out of her mind for the time being. "Meanwhile, you concentrate on creating a fantastic event."

She rolled her eyes with a dramatic gesture. "You're asking the impossible. Our simple showing has turned into a who's who of the rich and famous. An intimate performance by Alexander Summers made my event the 'must have an invitation' event of the year for Santa Fe. How did I let you talk me into this?"

"First of all, did you really expect Alex to stay

away after he found out about your connection with La Guitarra? Besides, we *want* this to be 'the event of the year'—or did you forget?"

"Of course not. I want it to be a success, but did everyone have to come? I mean I understand Lara Fallon is Alex's fiancée. He couldn't very well leave her behind. But why is Daniel Fallon coming too?"

"Of all our guests, he's the one I'd like to see the most."

He could see his comment surprised her.

"Daniel is like a second father to me. Of all people, I want him to see this and to meet you, to know I'm doing well. It'll make him happy to know things are working out for me."

A small frown creased her brow.

"Now what?"

She shrugged. "Are you sure you're not just trying to make up for the past?"

Brett caught his breath. Rafaela had a way of making him uncomfortable. In the beginning, finding the source of the Chaco pitcher had been his goal. But very soon, it turned to keeping Rafaela safe. He doubted she would understand that right now, not without the whole explanation, and there wasn't time. Fortunately, the gallery's phone rang and distracted her from getting an answer.

Rafaela climbed to her feet. Brett followed her. Just as she picked up the receiver, Emilio came in with a box of programs.

Brett waved. "You're early."

"Looks like we're about to get hit with this afternoon's shower. I wanted to get all this valuable paper inside before it did."

Brett glanced at Rafaela. "I'm glad you're here. I'd

like to talk to you." He motioned to the back showroom with his head. With a casual wave to Rafaela, Emilio followed.

Alone with the young man, Brett explained his concerns. "Rafaela's convinced that Angie's behind the situations, but I'm not."

Emilio shook his head. "She's more responsible than you know." He glanced to the door and lowered his voice. "I didn't want to tell Rafaela unless I had to, but Angie's mental."

"Anyone who would carry a grudge so long has some serious issues."

"No, man. I mean she's really mental, as in…institutional."

"You mean she has a psychological condition?"

Emilio nodded. "Her last year of college she had a complete breakdown and her parents had to have her committed for treatment. Heavy-duty meds helped her get things under control, and they released her. Her parents financed the gallery to help get her on her feet. For the first couple of years, things went great, but in the last year things have started to slip again."

"Are you sure about this?"

"Positive. She's also mixing alcohol with those meds, and that's dangerous. One night she showed up on my front yard screaming crazy things, crying about how we should never have broken up. But worse, she said some dangerous things about Rafaela. I brought her in and sobered her up. She fell asleep on my couch and the next morning didn't remember a thing."

"That's disturbing news."

Emilio nodded. "I didn't want to say anything to Rafaela. She's had enough on her plate, but I've kept my eye on Angie ever since. Rafaela saw us and thought we were getting involved, but the truth is, I've been keeping close tabs on Angie. I didn't know about the accidents, though. I guess I should have paid more attention."

"You paid more than enough attention. Now that we know the truth, our biggest concern should be the showing. Angie won't miss an opportunity to create some real damage."

"Don't worry—I've got it covered. I called in my cousins. One or the other of us has been following Angie for the past week. We know where she is every minute, day and night. And we've already set up guards for the evening of the event. Five different cars will be stationed around the plaza and driving up and down the street. Rafaela's event will go on without a hitch."

Brett grinned and clapped Emilio on the shoulder. "Remind me never to get on the bad side of the Hastings clan."

Emilio grinned back. "Good idea, man. Good idea."

~*~

Rafaela closed her eyes.

Alexander Summers's lyrical Flamenco rhythms floated through her small gallery. Seated on a high stool in one corner, the lights dimmed except for one small spotlight, he created musical magic that flowed in and around the crowd like a soft caress.

In her mind, it was *her* caress. As if she was saying, "*Welcome to my dream.*"

Everything was perfect. Alex's music. The soft lights. The beautiful artwork around them, Brett's

149

hand in hers. Perfect. She could not have planned a more ideal showing. She never thought she would showcase the Madrigals's work or that Alex Summers would sing at one of her events. Not in her wildest imagination. She never dared dream this big.

Maybe God saw things differently.

A scripture from Ephesians 3:20 popped into her mind. *Now all glory to God, who is able, through his mighty power at work within us to accomplish infinitely more than we might ask or think.*

The quote had stuck in her mind, but she'd never really understood it, or believed it. Until today. The Lord had looked into her heart and given her more than she'd ever dreamed possible. More than she knew she wanted or needed. His power *was* mighty.

Alex ended his song. Her guests clapped in appreciation. They'd sent out sixty invitations to her most valued customers, members of the press and a few Santa Fe officials. Almost everyone on the list had responded. The gallery was full, and she'd already received offers on two of Emilio's pieces and a check for the Madrigals's most expensive piece.

The commission she'd get from the sales would be wonderful, but more than that, she was glad to open her gallery, to share her vision, and to have it so well-received by her peers and the people she loved.

Only one person was missing. Tío Aaron had come early and left shortly after. He and her mother had argued again.

Rafaela had seen him stalk away and noted her mother's frustrated expression.

"I'm so sorry, Mama."

She gave an abrupt shake of her head. "It's as if he's trying to pick a fight with me."

Rafaela clasped her hand. "Please don't let it ruin your evening."

Her mother smiled, her expression rueful. "It won't. I know we owe Aaron. He's done so much for us, but frankly, with his help comes a sense of obligation. Somehow he always leaves me feeling as if I'm beholden to him. I never feel that way with Brett." She patted Rafaela's hand. "It's been good to have that young man here. It's helped me to recognize Aaron's negativity." Smiling, she squeezed Rafaela's hand. "It's time to put all that behind us, mija. Tonight is the beginning of a new chapter in our lives."

Before Rafaela could respond, Daniel Fallon joined them. "Excuse me, Mrs. de Silva. I've been looking for a moment to speak with you. I believe my wife and I saw you perform in New York back some years ago."

Her mother's lips parted in surprise. "Yes, yes, I was there. It was my last performance in public. Rafaela was born the next year."

Rafaela watched the two of them in amazement. A widow and a widower, reminiscing and laughing about the past and their partners. After a while, Rafaela realized her presence was not needed. Smiling, she slipped away.

Daniel Fallon had not left her mother's side since. In fact, he stood beside her now, across the way from Rafaela.

Alex's last song wound down. The guests began to clap and cheer as he rose from the stool and took a bow.

Brett slipped away to raise the lights.

Rafaela extended her hand to thank Alex, and he pulled her in for a quick hug. Then she turned to face her guests. "That concludes the evening's activities.

Thank you all so much for coming and sharing this wonderful night with us. Please feel free to browse. The Madrigals, Mr. Gonzales, and I will be happy to answer any questions. Again, thank you for sharing this amazing event with us."

A low murmur broke over the group as guests began to chat. Others gathered their things.

Rafaela stood near the door, thanking the attendees and answering questions, but she was still close enough to overhear Brett and Daniel Fallon's conversation a few feet away.

"Brett, what a great event. I haven't enjoyed myself so much in…well, I don't know how long. But it's also an incredible discovery. Once again, you've proven you have talent for good business. I hope this was your way of telling me you've had enough time away and are ready to come back to work. Your position is open to you anytime."

"Thank you, Daniel. I've wanted to hear that for a long time."

Brett's response made Rafaela's heart skip a beat. They turned away so she wasn't able to hear the next words. They moved to the corner but stood talking in quiet tones for a long while. Each minute chipped away at Rafaela's calm.

What did Brett mean? Did he hope to return to New York? Did he think she would go with him? And most importantly, had he planned all this, hoping a job offer would be the outcome? Did he use this event—her and her family—to get back in Fallon's good graces?

She didn't want to jump to conclusions, but the longer they stayed in the corner talking, the more uncertain she became. Now she couldn't wait for the event to end so she could discuss it with Brett.

At last, her guests departed. All that remained were her small group of friends and family. She locked the front door and started toward the group. The caterers had finished loading their supplies, and Brett led them to the back door.

Daniel and Lara Fallon, her mother, Emilio, and Troy and Eliza all stood by the small easel holding Sofia's painting. True to her word, Rafaela had exhibited her sister's rendition of the damaged front gates.

Troy gestured to the painting.

"Look at these strokes. She has a style much more advanced than her age. She's an ideal candidate for the school."

Sofia at the Fallon School of Art. Terror raced through Rafaela. Her sister had come a long way in the last few weeks, but she would never survive at the school. The change would be too much. The competition would send her into bouts of binging and purging. Surely her mother knew that. Surely she'd put a stop to the suggestion right here and now.

Troy pointed to the painting again. "Look at her shading."

Her mother nodded. "Sofia is very talented, like her father."

"Her father!" Eliza's exclamation startled them all. "I'd almost forgotten. I have to show you what the girls and I discovered while we were cleaning." She hurried to the back room where they stored the canvases and came out carrying her father's portrait of her grandfather.

"Look at this, Troy." She turned the painting around.

"That's my pitcher!" He turned to her mother. "Who is this?"

"It's my father-in-law. My husband painted this many years ago. His father found that piece of pottery on our property when he was young. What did you mean, it's your pitcher?"

"I bought it a little over a year ago."

"Rafaela was forced to sell it. We never knew who the buyer was. It's so good to know it's in good hands."

"Yes, well it cost me more than it's worth."

Her mother frowned. "What do you mean?"

"This pitcher almost cost us our freedom. Its style and markings are very similar to a group of pieces that appeared on the black market. The I.C.E. found out about my pitcher and thought the school was involved in the trafficking of illegal artifacts. If it wasn't for Alex and Lara's hard work, we'd probably all be in jail now."

Shock swept through Rafaela. Her grandfather's pitcher had implicated Brett and all his friends and colleagues in the black market scheme...a scheme where the authorities were still searching for the source and hoping to catch the leaders of the operation.

Cold realization swept through Rafaela. Her grandfather's pitcher might be the link the authorities needed to find that source and to arrest the leaders. If Brett was instrumental in solving the crime, he might finally feel exonerated.

Had he seen the painting and recognized the pitcher? If he had seen it, why did he keep the information from her?

She could think of only one reason he would do that. Admitting he recognized the pitcher would expose his secrets and the ulterior motives behind his offers to help her family…maybe even his declarations of love.

At that moment, Brett returned from escorting the caterers out.

The group turned almost in unison.

Troy pointed to the picture. "Brett, did you know about this?"

Brett's crestfallen expression told Rafaela all she needed to know. With one simple look, her perfect world crashed down around her.

14

Rain fell in a steady drizzle down the galley window. All afternoon the dark clouds and constant rainfall had turned an already difficult day into torture for Rafaela.

Last night after the showing, she'd refused to ride home with Brett, even to talk to him. After a sleepless night, she rose early and drove her truck into town. She would have texted him and asked him not to come in at all, but opening the show to the public would create a steady flow of customers, and with Jan still out, she needed help.

Brett showed up promptly at eight. He shook his umbrella outside the door and closed it even as a couple dashed under the portico. He couldn't leave them standing in the rain so he gestured them inside and glanced at Rafaela at the desk.

She shrugged her agreement to opening early and greeted the customers.

The rain didn't slow the flow of traffic in and out of the gallery throughout the day. The newspaper had run a glowing article on the previous night's event, and customers, some paying but most not, came to see what the buzz was about.

Any other time, Rafaela would have been pleased, but today, instead of potential customers, she saw muddy prints being tracked all over her freshly cleaned gallery. She heard a million annoying questions when all she really wanted to do was crawl into a corner of her bedroom, wrap up in a blanket, and watch the rainfall.

She needed time to think and to pray before she spoke to Brett. She wanted to understand, to be reasonable, but couldn't forget the sense that something was not right. She thought of all the times she'd searched his gaze and found hidden shadows and secrets. She should have trusted her instincts. Should have known better. Should never have fallen in love.

In reality, Brett had done wonderful things for her family and her business. She appreciated all that, and could never repay him for his efforts. What she couldn't forgive was how he kept facts from her—for lying. She couldn't forgive him for manipulating her when she'd told him so many times how much she wanted honesty. But most of all, she couldn't forgive him for not being perfect, not being the man she thought him to be. Because she'd fallen in love with *that* man, and he didn't exist.

Rafaela had struggled with disillusionment for so long she thought she'd defeated it, but now that it had resurfaced, she didn't have the strength to do battle. All her effort went into smiling for her customers when she felt like crying. She had nothing left for anything else.

So when Laurie walked in the door after lunch, Rafaela groaned out loud.

Brett heard and moved closer, planting his legs, as if he were ready for action, ready to help if she needed him.

But she couldn't afford to accept his help. Not anymore. She needed to stand on her own two feet.

Taking a deep breath, she straightened her spine and turned to face her ex-friend.

In spite of the dreary day, Laurie wore large round sunglasses and her brown hair was pulled back in a severe bun at the nape of her neck. She wore a simple outfit: jeans and a light sweater. Everything about her was subdued.

Rafaela's greeting was less than warm and Laurie almost visibly winced.

"I'm sorry…" Rafaela began.

Laurie stopped her with a hand on her arm. "Don't. Don't apologize. I understand. My behavior the last few months, well, let's just say I wasn't thinking clearly. My marriage…"

Rafaela grasped the hand on her arm. "It's all right, Laurie. I know and understand."

She nodded and dipped her head. "Thanks. I appreciate that." Licking her lips, she looked up. "I've been trying to call the last few days to warn you…"

"Warn me?"

Laurie nodded then slid off the sunglasses. She had a deep purple bruise beneath one eye.

"Oh, no! Did Jeremy do that?"

"No. In fact, Jeremy saved me."

"From who?"

"Angie. I made the mistake of saying I was happy for you. She went berserk and attacked me. Jeremy pulled her off and took me to the emergency room."

Rafaela stared at the bruise, momentarily unable to speak. Finally she managed to force a few words past her tight throat. "Laurie, I'm so sorry."

"It's all right, really. I wasn't hurt that badly. Jeremy insisted we visit the hospital and file charges against her. He said it was important for your sake."

"My sake?"

Laurie nodded. "He says it's important to document Angie's attitude toward you in case...well, in case she does something crazy. She's absolutely gone wild where you're concerned."

Rafaela shook her head. "I don't understand why. She has everything. Her gallery is successful."

"Successful? Who told you that?"

"I—I guess I just assumed."

"Her business is going under, Rafe. The only reason she's stayed open this long is because her parents have been paying the bills. But that stopped about six months ago. They told her they wouldn't pay another dime toward her business unless she stopped drinking and went back to therapy. But then someone else picked up her expenses."

"Who would do that?"

"I don't know. She would never say, but it's someone with lots of money to blow because her business is a lost cause. She's driven away all her customers. Even her anonymous benefactor stopped supporting her about a month ago. Her condition has deteriorated so much, she's barely rational. And she's developed this thing about you, blames you for all of her problems. She's unstable, and I wanted you to know. I wish I had better news or could do more."

Rafaela squeezed her hands. "Thanks, Laurie. You helped more than you know by filing those charges. Thank Jeremy for me."

"I will. He's been my rock."

Laurie's words reminded Rafaela of what she'd just lost. A partner, someone to count on and to always be there. A pang of envy swept through her.

"This whole thing has actually drawn Jeremy and

me closer together. I'm going to Denver with him right after this. We may even move there."

"I'm glad for that." Rafaela hugged her friend, surprised at how much she meant the words. It comforted her to know God could draw some good out of this sorrow.

"I really am happy for you, Rafe. But please, please be careful. Angie isn't done yet."

~*~

The last customer exited the gallery and Brett locked the door behind him.

Rafaela focused on mopping up the muddy footprints dotting the floor. She studiously avoided his gaze.

He took the mop from her hands. "Go ahead and close out the cash. I'll finish this."

By the time he'd dumped the dirty water and hung the mop in the back, Rafaela had deposited the small change in the safe and locked it. Still, she wouldn't look at him.

He leaned against the doorjamb and folded his arms. "You can avoid me as long as you want, but eventually we will talk."

She sighed. "What is there to say?"

"How about I'm sorry? I didn't mean to keep the information about the pitcher from you. It's just..." He gestured around the room. "We've been kind of busy around here."

"We were never so busy that you couldn't find the time to tell me something as important as this."

"You had enough to worry about."

"Well, now I have one more thing to worry about.

How to protect my family against someone so charming and so untrustworthy."

He hung his hands on his hips and closed his eyes. "*This* is why I didn't tell you. I was afraid you'd react this way, that you wouldn't believe me no matter what I said."

She shook her head. "So now your dishonesty is my fault?"

"Of course not! I should have told you. I already apologized for that, and I will apologize again. I'm sorry. But I didn't do it to be deceitful. I did it because I was afraid you would freeze me out, like you're doing right now."

"I heard your conversation with Daniel, Brett. He offered your old job to you."

"Yeah, so?" He raised his shoulders in a question.

"You said you'd been waiting a long time to hear that."

"I have. I needed to know Daniel still had confidence in me. That didn't mean I was going to accept his offer."

"Are you telling me you didn't do all of this to get back in his good graces, to get your old life back?"

Her words hurt so deeply, he couldn't speak for a long while. "I did this, Rafaela, to get back in my own good graces...and God's." His voice was raspy. "I asked Him to make me useful, to find a purpose for my life. I thought I found it here with you."

She folded her arms and looked at the window where the rain streamed down the pane in rivulets. Finally, she shook her head and turned back to him. "I'm sorry, Brett. I don't think I can share my life with a man who's afraid to be honest with me, who manipulates my life to hide from the truth. I lived like that with my father, and I can't do it again." She said it with such finality.

Cold trickled through him. The wall had come up again and the windows were shuttered against him. He could see it in her face, in the way she held her body rigid and untouchable.

Just like that, he was out.

Didn't she realize she'd just proven him right? He had good reason to fear her reaction. After all that had passed between them, she'd closed herself off to him, because of one mistake.

Their happy time. The passion. It was over.

Lucia's words came back to him. She'd placed her faith in her husband instead of God. And when her husband failed, as all men do, it destroyed her world. Her daughter was making the same mistake.

"You're right. I'm a man—a frail, simple man who makes mistakes just like your father."

She took a deep breath then nodded slowly. "Yes, he was frail and weak. I was wrong to put so much trust in him. I won't make that mistake again."

"Your mistake wasn't in loving your father. It was in loving him *more* than God."

Her features hardened. "You think God is punishing me for loving my father?"

Slowly, he shook his head. "You are a gift in my life, Rafaela. I thought you felt the same. I didn't realize I was a punishment."

Her lips parted. But she didn't deny it. Didn't speak at all. An icy wave swept over him, filling every inch of his being, even into his fingertips and toes.

All the love he'd showered on her, all the care and understanding had never even touched her. Her heart was hidden so deep and so far behind her self-constructed walls, he didn't know if anyone would ever reach her. Not even God.

That's when he knew it was hopeless.

He looked around as if just waking from a dream. He gathered his thoughts. "Tell your mother I won't be there for dinner tonight. Tell her...I don't know. Make some excuse. There's no need to upset everyone in the house. Tomorrow Troy and Eliza will be on their way home. After they leave, I'll pack my things and be out of your studio by evening. I won't bother you again."

He turned and walked out the back door. In the short distance to his car, the steady rainfall drenched him. He slid inside, mindless of his wet clothes or the water dripping off his head. He started the engine and pulled away from the gallery. Stopping at the intersection, he looked right and left, with no idea where he was going. When a car behind him honked, he turned right simply to get out of the way.

The rain had washed the quaint downtown streets of Santa Fe clean. He drove through the twisting lanes, stopping for pedestrians, slowing to look at Pueblo style homes, gardens and shops tucked behind stylish stucco fences and bright-colored gates.

This would be the last time he would drive these streets, see the unique places, the Spanish style he'd come to love. In a few days, he'd leave and he would never come back. Santa Fe would hold too many memories.

Where would he go now? What would he do?

He'd come so far. Learned so much. He never expected to be in this place of emptiness again. And yet, here he was.

Six months ago he'd made the same choices, driven away from his life without a backward glance.

But then, the future held hope, possibilities. What lay ahead was better than what he left behind. Now, everything he wanted would be behind him. He had no future. No hope.

He drove aimlessly until the sun set. The streets grew dark, and the rush hour traffic thinned. Still chilled, he turned on the heater. But the cold didn't come from his damp clothes. It came from a deep dread.

He turned his car down a residential street and climbed a hill. Lights shone out of a building at the top of the hill and he drove to it, drawn like a moth to a flame. Catching the light he'd followed, raindrops sparkled on his windshield, like a winking welcome.

The building was a church. The parking lot was full, but Brett found a space. He parked and hurried inside. A service was going on. People were singing. Brett sat in the back pew and let the songs of praise and worship wash over his aching heart.

Like a healing balm, the music flowed over him, eased his soul. By the time the service ended, God's warmth filled him.

He wasn't alone. Unlike Rafaela, he had faith. He knew the Lord had led him here. God would lead Brett where he needed to go. He would not abandon him.

Filled with peace, he returned to his car. He drove through the hills, seeing more sights, saying goodbye to a new friend, and packing away the images to treasure later.

Well past midnight, he drove into the horseshoe drive of the rancho. Easing open the gates, he slipped past a dark house and hurried to the studio. He stripped down, showered, put on pajama bottoms, and slid into bed. Clasping his hands behind his head, he stared up at the dark ceiling and prayed over and over again.

He must have dozed because the next time he opened his eyes, someone was pounding on his door. Drowsy, he stumbled his way through the dark and opened it.

Christie and Sofia stood in the doorway. Sofia grabbed his hand as soon as she saw him, her eyes as wide as saucers.

"Brett, Mama sent me to get you. The police called. The gallery is on fire."

He grasped her shoulders. "I'll be right there."

Dashing inside, he dressed in his jeans and a T-shirt, scooped up his keys and wallet, and hit the door at a dead run. He reached the courtyard just as Rafaela came out of the house. She'd dressed the same way, in jeans and T-shirt. Her purse hung over her shoulder and she was looping her long hair in a rubber band.

They moved in unison out the gate, but he beat Rafaela to his car and started the engine. When she headed for her truck, he stuck one leg out and rose to shout over the hood of his vehicle.

"We don't have time for this nonsense. Get in."

She hesitated, but only for a moment. Then she dashed across, jerked open the door and climbed in. Brett screeched out of the driveway, spraying dirt and gravel behind.

He waited until they'd climbed out of the valley and were on the four-lane road before he asked his questions. "Did the police tell you anything?"

"Only that there was a fire. They have it under control but there's been damage."

Trepidation filled Brett. "To the art work or the building?"

"I don't know." Her voice trembled, and Brett knew she feared the same thing he did. If the artwork was damaged, all of the money from last night's showing would have to be returned. Months, maybe years of Emilio's work would be destroyed and have to be compensated.

Brett was almost afraid to ask his next question. "You do have insurance, don't you?"

He glanced over to see her slight nod. "Yes, but I didn't think…everything was happening so fast I didn't ask for an increase. I have the minimum coverage, and my deductible."

She didn't say the rest. She didn't need to. The deductible would be high. She might be able to come up with the money but she had the expenses from the showing and now no profits to pay them back.

This fire could destroy her business and force her into bankruptcy.

"Don't worry." The words seemed inadequate but they were all he could think to say. "I'm sure Troy and Eliza have their own insurance."

She nodded. "Probably. But Emilio…"

Her last thought trailed off, leaving them both with a silence that said it all.

Brett hit the gas pedal, and the sports car leapt forward. He was forced to slow once they reached the rain-slicked streets of town. He didn't want to skid out. Rafaela chafed at the slower speed and leaned forward in her seat, straining to see ahead.

When they turned the final corner to the plaza, a fire engine blocked their way. Brett hit the brakes and parked in the middle of the street. Rafaela jumped out of the car and ran toward the fire engine with Brett close behind.

As soon as they came around the corner, they both stopped short. The scene in front of them was worse than Brett had imagined. The plate glass store window had been shattered. On the sidewalk in front of the window lay a huge sledgehammer covered in blood.

"Someone broke in." Rafaela's shocked tone matched Brett's own feelings.

Huge fire hoses crossed the ground in front of them and snaked through the window and appeared to be stretched all the way to the back show room where the art was located.

Rafaela groaned and reached a hand out to Brett for support. He grabbed it and wrapped an arm around her shoulder.

"Are you the owner?"

Rafaela's moment of weakness lasted only a second. She pushed out of Brett's embrace and moved toward the fireman. "I am, yes."

He gestured to the building. "As you can see, the perpetrator broke the front window and moved quickly to the back. Fortunately, the alarms went off immediately and the police were dispatched. She made it to the back, doused some of the artwork in gasoline and fired them up. Again, your alarm systems performed well and we arrived quickly. We were able to put out the fire and save most of the artwork."

Rafaela nodded like a woman in a trance. "She. You said she."

The fireman pointed back behind them.

They'd been so concerned with the gallery they hadn't looked down the street.

Angie Morrow was strapped to a gurney about to be loaded in an ambulance. Her arms and legs were bloodied. Smoke blackened her blue dress and her head hung limply to one side.

"She was lucky the alarms worked like they were supposed to." The fire chief shook his head. "Once she started the fire, she sat on the ground and watched it. We found her unconscious when we arrived."

"How is she?"

"I'm no doctor, but like I said, we got here pretty quickly. Smoke inhalation for sure. Some of the cuts on her feet and legs from stepping through the window look pretty bad. Other than that, I think she'll survive."

Brett took a deep breath. "You said you saved most of the art work. What was damaged?"

"The two small pieces she doused in gasoline. They went up quickly and are destroyed. We think the rest are in pretty good shape."

Brett stretched his shoulders, trying to ease the tension away. Emilio.

Angie had targeted Emilio's work. In her unstable condition, she'd fixated on Rafaela and Emilio. Now she'd taken action.

Had the showing and Rafaela's success pushed Angie over the edge? Or was it something else? Laurie had said Angie's anonymous backer had stopped paying her expenses. Who was this backer? Why was he or she anonymous, and why did they suddenly stop supporting Angie?

This secretive arrangement bothered him. Surely this person knew Angie was unstable. If they cared for her, why wouldn't they come forward or find her help unless...

Unless Angie's unstable condition worked to their advantage. Maybe her mysterious supporter knew her fixation on Rafaela and encouraged it, driving Angie over the brink and plunging her into desperate action.

Brett was convinced Angie wasn't the original attacker. She was just a pawn in the relentless, secret campaign against Rafaela.

Who was it and what would they do next? Every act brought more danger to Rafaela and everything she loved.

A frisson of alarm shivered up his back. Lucia and Sofia. He pulled out his cellphone and dialed the ranch's number.

Lucia answered and some of his concern eased. He relayed the information about the gallery. She in turn, relayed the information to Troy and Eliza who had risen when the police called and opted to stay and support her.

Brett said a silent thanks to Troy and his wise actions.

"How is Rafaela?" Lucia's voice was fraught with concern.

Brett glanced across the way to Rafaela who was giving her report to the fireman. She looked tired but straight, tall, and totally independent.

"She's a pillar of strength."

"Why doesn't that comfort me?"

"I guess we both know why."

She sighed. "Yes, I'm afraid we do."

There was silence on the phone for a moment. "Thanks for letting me know what's going on. I think I can reassure the girls now and send them to bed."

As soon as he hung up, he texted Troy. *Stay alert. Something's not right.* Troy texted back an OK.

Next Brett tried to call Emilio but got no answer. Why wasn't he answering and where was the cousin who was supposed to be watching Angie?

The fireman finished his report with Rafaela and

crossed to Brett. He asked about alarms and the condition of the gallery when Brett had left earlier in the day. When the fireman finished, Brett had to answer police questions about Angie's threats. By the time the interviews were over and the fire crew had finally cleared their equipment, the sun was peeking over the distant mountains.

Rafaela stood beside him as they thanked the firemen and watched them pull away. Together, they watched the distant sky turn from gray to mauve to pink. The beautiful colors reminded him of the day he'd watched Rafaela run over the rise, a day full of promise for him. He glanced her way, hoping...he didn't know what.

The sunrise touched Rafaela too. He could see it in the pain etched deep in her features. Why this beautiful scene and the memory of their first meeting caused her such pain, he wasn't sure. But he was fairly certain something dark was churning behind that hurt. Something more than his lack of judgment in keeping his knowledge of the pitcher to himself. That certainty put him on edge.

Crossing her arms tight, she moved toward the broken doorway of the gallery. "I'm going to see if I can get through to my insurance company."

Brett moved to follow her, but someone called his name.

Emilio jogged up the sidewalk toward him.

Brett hurried to meet him. "Where have you been? I've called several times."

"We were at the hospital with my cousin, Art."

"Not the one watching Angie?"

Emilio nodded. "When he started dozing off, he called his brother for help, told him a friend had dropped by with a latte laced with something. By the time we got there, he was out cold and we couldn't revive him. We took him to the emergency room."

"Is he OK?"

"Yeah. They did a blood test. His friend put sleeping pills in his drink."

"Did Art tell you the name of this friend?"

"His name's Bert and as far as we know, he has no connection with Angie or Rafaela. But his mother did admit he came into a lot of money a few days ago."

"His mother admitted that?"

"Yeah, we went straight to his house. Bert wasn't there, but his mother was ticked when we told her what happened. She's very traditional. It made her angry that Bert took money to hurt a fellow tribe member."

"Did she tell you where he went?"

Emilio grinned. "She even gave us the address. She's sure he went to Taos to his girlfriend's house. My cousins are on their way now. When they get there, we'll find out who put Bert up to this."

Brett sighed. "I hope so. Whoever it is holds all the cards. He's always two steps ahead of us and doesn't seem to care how much damage he causes."

15

Eight o'clock brought a steady stream of onlookers to the front of the store. Rafaela's insurance company advised her not to touch anything until the adjustor arrived later in the day, so she wasn't able to sweep or clean inside. But the plate glass outside on the sidewalk was a hazard, especially with so many people stopping by.

Brett and Emilio helped her clean it up; then the two of them took Emilio's truck to pick up plywood to cover the door and window.

Her mother and the Madrigals came about mid-morning. They brought rolls and coffee in the nick of time.

Rafaela was beginning to feel the aftereffects of her shock. She was teary and weak, and every time Brett looked at her, she had to resist the urge to throw herself into his arms and cry. She couldn't do that. Not now, maybe not ever. She had to stand strong. Had to do what was right.

The destruction of her gallery was her undoing. It sent her world spinning. The gallery was her security. Everything hinged on it—Her ability to care for her mother and sister. Her standing in the community. Her hard work. Gone. Destroyed by someone she had once called a friend.

Worse, that friend had almost lost her own life and most certainly her mind. Seeing Angie on that gurney, bleeding and senseless had shaken Rafaela to the core. She remembered how tenuous life could be, and that thought sent her spiraling back to the dark days right after her father's death.

She never wanted to go back to those days. She would do anything to see that the darkness never happened again.

Brett's mistake paled in the face of the tragedy unfolding around her. She could forgive him, but she couldn't afford to rely on him. She couldn't collapse in his arms and let him take care of her. She had to stand on her own two feet and do what she should have done long ago. With grim certainty, she affirmed those thoughts even as the others laughed at something Sofia said.

Her mother edged close. "Are you sure you're all right?"

"I'm fine." She sipped her coffee. "Just tired."

Her mother hugged her. Her body resisted the comfort, feeling stiff and unbending even in her mother's embrace.

Frowning, her mother stepped away. "Aaron called. He's in Albuquerque. His office just gave him the news. He said he'd be here later today."

"Good." Rafaela nodded then walked over to where the Madrigals were examining their work.

"It's amazing how much heat the piece took without damage."

Eliza laughed. "Well, it has been heat-fired once, Troy."

He pulled her into a hug. "Only you could make a joke on a morning like this."

Any other time, their loving playfulness would have made Rafaela happy. Today it poked her like a sharp object, reminding her to be strong.

Her mother herded the girls toward the front door. "I think we're in the way here. We'll go now. Rafaela?"

She looked up.

"Come home as soon as you see the adjustor. You need to rest."

Rafaela nodded and then said goodbye to the Madrigals. Sighing, she walked back into the gallery. All she wanted was the adjustor to come so she could finish her business.

Another group came to the window, asking their curious questions. When will the exhibit be open again? Was anyone hurt? Rafaela answered as politely as she could, but she was getting tired of their well-meaning curiosity.

Brett and Emilio returned and leaned a large piece of wood against the wall. As soon as the visitors left, she turned to the men. "I'm beginning to feel like the newest circus act in town."

"We'll have this up soon and you can relax." Brett's assurance did little to ease the tightness holding her body prisoner.

The insurance adjustor arrived just after the locksmith. Brett spoke with the locksmith while Rafaela followed the adjustor around the store. His examination was thorough and complete. When he finished, he turned to Rafaela.

"I have the police report and a good estimate of the damage. Of course, you're the victim here. We'll cover all the damage. As soon as we finalized the claim, we'll release the funds, less your ten thousand dollar deductible."

Rafaela nodded as he continued to talk, but his words blurred. She knew the deductible was high. Had signed the paperwork. But for some unexplainable reason, she'd needed to hear him say the words. Needed the confirmation for her next move.

"Here's my card with my office address. If you get the money to me by tomorrow morning, I can have the workers out here by afternoon. We'll have you back in business as soon as possible, Ms. de Silva."

She nodded again and took the card, barely remembering to thank him.

The locksmith had finished, but Brett still stood at the door. He opened it for the adjustor and closed it behind the man. As soon as he was out the door, Emilio shook his head. "Ten thousand dollar deductible? What were you thinking, Rafaela? Why in the world would you agree to that high amount?"

She didn't answer. Couldn't.

Brett answered for her. "The higher the deductible, the lower the monthly payments. It's better to have a high deductible and some insurance than none at all."

"I couldn't afford more and cover the utilities here and at home." Home. Soon, she wouldn't even have that.

"Rafaela, I can loan you the money for the deductible."

Her gaze shot to Brett. "You have that kind of money just laying around?"

"Not just laying around, no. But I have enough to make you a loan."

She closed her eyes and shook her head. "No, Brett. I can't take it. I can't depend on anyone anymore. I have to do this on my own."

"OK. So you're going to do it on your own. Where are you going to get the money?" Emilio was still frowning.

"I'm going to sell my property to Tío Aaron. The house belongs to my mother but my father left the land to me. If I sell it, I'll have the money I need, and I'll owe no one."

They were both stunned into silence.

Then Emilio said something beneath his breath and turned away.

Brett shook his head. "You'd rather sell your heritage than take help from a friend."

Rafaela stared at him. Had she heard him correctly? "Is that what you think I'm doing? I take help from my friends over and over again. They've done enough. My heritage isn't more important to me than my friends and family, and it's time I proved it."

"By selling what we've all worked so hard to help you keep." Emilio's face was a mask of confusion.

"Don't you see? That's the problem. So many times Tío Aaron offered to buy the rancho, to make life easier for my mother. But my father couldn't bear to part with his land. And now I've been doing the same thing. Hanging on when Sofia needs better health care and my mother—she's suffered enough. Now my friends are paying, too. Brett, all those hours you spent working. The Madrigals took a chance bringing their exhibit here for nothing. And you, Emilio, you've lost everything. I can't allow my friends to support me any longer. I need to stop it now. I need to be stronger than my father and do what's right."

"This is crazy." Emilio was agitated. "You're not in your right mind. Aaron won't do it. He won't buy your land when you're in this state."

"He'll buy it." Brett's voice was low, taut and tense. "He'll snatch it up in a heartbeat." He focused his intense green-tinted gaze on Rafaela. "Don't do this. It's a mistake."

"You of all people should know how important independence is to me."

He nodded slowly. "I know. That's why I'm asking you not to do it. I don't want my bad judgment to push you into giving up what's most important to you."

She swallowed. "This has nothing to do with you or what happened between us. This is me, taking care of my family and doing what's right."

Brett glared at her for a long while. Then he tossed the door keys to Emilio, who caught them one handed.

"See that she gets home safely. I don't want to be around when Pomeroy gets here."

He spun and stalked out.

16

From the rise of a hill just outside Santa Fe, Brett watched another mauve and purple sunset with his cup of coffee balanced on the steering wheel.

Rafaela's decision was wrong on so many levels. No matter what she said, she was headed in the wrong direction and he knew their differences had pushed her down that path.

He didn't know how to reach her or even where to begin. One thing he knew for certain. Pomeroy would snatch up her land. Whether he saw it as a way to get closer to Lucia or simply as a means to make Rafaela and her family more beholden to him, Pomeroy *would* buy the land.

The thought turned the coffee in his stomach to acid. Rafaela's land was a part of who she was, like her dancing. She belonged there. She needed it. Selling it was the wrong thing.

And she completely ignored the fact that someone was still trying to hurt her. He was sure of it. But without proof, he would never convince her that Angie was not the sole cause of her accidents.

His cellphone buzzed. "Hello."

"How are you?" Alex's deep voice was somehow reassuring.

Brett shook his head. "Don't ask."

"You're safe, aren't you? They caught the woman who started the fire."

"We're safe from Angie, but I don't think she's the one behind all of this."

"Well, besides calling to see about your condition, my friends at I.C.E. asked me to check in with you. They appreciated your tip about Pomeroy."

"Did they turn up something on him?"

"Yes, in fact, he shot to the position of number one person of interest. They established a connection with Ferone. But then, Pomeroy must have gotten wind that they were investigating him because he started some unusual activities."

"What do you mean unusual?"

"Has he taken several business trips recently to Phoenix and Denver?"

"Yeah. What's so unusual about that?"

"He's selling off all his holdings. Everything. All his properties."

"Selling. That doesn't make any sense."

"It does if he's preparing to run. He's exhibiting all the signs of someone preparing to leave the country permanently. It's making my I.C.E. friends nervous."

"Leave the country…" A thousand thoughts flashed through Brett's mind. "There's been no indication on this end. Are you sure it's not financial trouble? Does he need the cash?"

"Not from what they can tell. He's selling out and depositing his assets overseas."

"You said he sold his holdings in Phoenix and Denver. What about his property in Albuquerque? Did he sell that?"

Brett heard the ruffling of paper on the other end. Then Alex said, "I don't see any record here of a trip to Albuquerque."

"He was there. Lucia drove down and picked him

up in his car."

"He flew in?"

"I imagine so. He was in Phoenix. He'd loaned her his car and so he asked for a ride home from Albuquerque. They made a day of it and went to dinner."

"If he flew, it would have shown up on this report. There's no mention of it."

"Maybe he rented a car."

"It would be listed. Cars, buses, train manifests are all here."

"So how did he get from Phoenix to Albuquerque?"

"Good question. You could always ask him."

Brett made a rude sound. "Not likely. He's busy right now accepting Rafaela's offer to buy her land."

Alex was silent. "Why would he buy her land and sell everything else? Doesn't sound much like a man preparing to run."

Hope blossomed in Brett. "Maybe he *is* preparing to leave. Maybe he refused her offer."

"I.C.E. would be very interested to know if he refused."

"So would I. I'll call and get back to you."

"Great. In the meantime, I'll have them check into this Albuquerque thing. Can you give me a date?"

"Let me see. I think it was the second week of August."

"Are you sure? Exact dates would help."

Brett considered for a moment. "Yeah, I'm sure. It was the day after Jan called…wait a minute."

Thoughts whirled through his bran and a sudden chill swept over him.

"What is it?" Alex's voice held a note of concern.

"Another one of Rafaela's 'accidents.' Rafaela's assistant Jan Hastings took a leave of absence to help her elderly parents in Albuquerque. Their home had a break-in, and it shook them up so badly it impacted their health. She couldn't leave them. Pomeroy was in Albuquerque when it happened."

"You think he had something to do with it?"

Brett watched the sun sink behind the hills before he answered. "It's beginning to make sense. Pomeroy is in close enough contact to tamper with Rafaela's shoes and her car. He was in Albuquerque when Jan's family was attacked, and with all these property sales, he has a lot of cash to throw at Angie and Bert."

"I know who Angie is, but who's Bert?"

Brett quickly explained Emilio's cousins. When he finished, Alex was silent for a long while.

"The Hastings cousins should have filed a police report. It would have helped. But what's the purpose of all these attacks? I don't see a motive."

Brett took a deep breath. "Pomeroy's been trying to buy Rafaela's land for years. All these accidents are geared to force her into financial difficulty so she'll have to sell."

"But why would he want her land if he's selling all his other property?"

"Because if he owns the land, he won't have to leave the country. He'll have the legal right to excavate all the Chaco artifacts he's been selling on the black market. If he's the owner, I.C.E. can't touch him."

Alex whistled. "And you said she's going to offer it to him tonight?"

"It's probably already happened. I've got to get to her, try to convince her not to sell."

"That will be hard. If Pomeroy is a life-long friend,

she won't want to believe you."

"It'll be harder than you think. We've...had some issues lately. I need to find some proof before it's too late."

"Brett, be careful. Pomeroy is a dangerous man, and you're already in his cross-hairs."

"He doesn't like me but the feeling's mutual."

"It's more than that. If he's been trying to drive Rafaela to financial ruin, you've been thwarting him every step of the way. He also knows someone's tipped off I.C.E. You're the most likely candidate. If he's preparing to run, he's a desperate man and desperate men are extremely volatile. Remember what happened when I took matters into my own hands. I almost got Lara killed."

Brett remembered all too well. The memory gave him pause. "What are you suggesting?"

"Let I.C.E. do their job. If he's guilty, they'll find the proof. Talk to Rafaela. Convince her to hold off on the sale until they have a chance to look into this more."

Brett sighed. "I'll try, Alex, but things are rough between us. I don't think she'll listen to me."

"Do your best. I'll get back to you as soon as I can." He rang off.

Brett stared into the night sky, trying to put all the pieces together. The puzzle hinged on one thing— whether or not Pomeroy accepted Rafaela's offer.

He dialed Emilio's number.

"About time I heard from you. Why'd you rush out like that?"

Brett didn't waste time trying to explain. "Did Pomeroy accept Rafaela's offer?"

Emilio sighed. "Yeah, he did. Surprised me. I

thought he cared about her more than that."

"He cares more about himself. In fact, I think he may be the one behind all this."

"Pomeroy?" Emilio paused. "Before today I wouldn't have believed it. Now I have to wonder."

"It's going to be harder to convince Rafaela."

"That's for sure."

"Did your cousins track down Bert?"

"They caught him in Taos. He says his boss paid him to take the drink to my cousin. A building contractor by the name of Jay Murphy."

"Does he have some connection with Pomeroy?"

"Not that we know of, but Pomeroy owns property everywhere and works with half a dozen contractors. Funny thing though, Bert's worked for Murphy for about a year. He says Murphy's got this sort of elite team that does special jobs for him."

"What kind of special jobs?"

"Heavy construction. Bert didn't know exactly what, but Murphy pays these guys almost double, and they work all kinds of crazy hours. Murphy told Bert he'd pay him to take this drink to my cousin. When he balked, Murphy offered him a spot on the team."

"Are you sure Bert doesn't know what the team does?"

"No, but Bert operates heavy equipment. Usually makes good money, but he's got problems with gambling."

"That explains why he was willing to drug his friend."

"He didn't know about the sleeping pills in the coffee. He swears he was just supposed to talk to my cousin, distract him so the woman could slip out. When Bert found out Art ended up in the hospital, he was freaked. He said he wasn't going back in to work. He was done with Murphy. But I told him he could help us more by staying put and keeping an eye on the place."

Brett nodded. "Thanks, Emilio. That was a great idea. Do me a favor, call my friend Alex and tell him what you've just told me. He's got connections and they're already investigating Pomeroy. Maybe they can dig up something with this Murphy."

"What are you going to do?"

"See if I can talk some sense into Rafaela."

"I hope you can."

"Thanks. I'll do my best." Brett clicked off and started his car. The roads were empty, so he pushed the speed limit and reached the rancho in record time.

Lights blazed in the house. Through the courtyard windows, he saw Lucia, Eliza, and Troy.

Rafaela was nowhere in sight. She must have gone straight to bed.

He didn't want to make the mistake again of not conferring with her first, so he texted her and asked her to meet him privately at the studio.

The lights in the studio were on, and he hurried across, hoping Rafaela might already be there. When he opened the door, Christie and Sofia popped up from the sofa.

"What are you two doing in here?"

"Waiting for you. We have something really important to tell you." Christie's face was so earnest, he almost groaned out loud. He hated to disappoint her, but his mind was too focused on his problem with Rafaela.

"Girls, I've had a really long day and I'm—"

"Please, Brett, this is really important and I'm

leaving tomorrow. We have to talk to you before then."

Brett sighed and plopped down on the couch. "OK. I'm all ears."

"The lights are real." Sofia spoke for the first time.

"What lights?"

"The ones that give Sofia nightmares. They're not imaginary," Christie said.

His gaze darted to Christie. Brett remembered the painting and nodded slowly. "I never thought they were."

"Christie saw them too."

"And I heard that monster growling...twice."

Brett's interest sank, and he leaned forward, linking his fingers between fingers. "Girls, we all know there are no monsters."

"Of course not." Christie nodded. "That's why the second time we heard it, we dressed and went out to investigate."

"What?" Brett scooted forward. "You two went out in the dark by yourselves?"

"We had to. No one would believe Sofia. We didn't think you'd believe me either." Christie folded her arms and Sofia nodded.

Brett ducked his head. "I didn't *not* believe you, Sofia. I saw your painting of the hill and I wanted to check it out. I've just kind of been busy."

"We know. That's one of the things that made us suspicious." Apparently, Sofia was gaining enough confidence to speak for herself. "The more I thought about it, the more I realized the noises only happened late at night or when all of the adults were gone."

"Yeah, and then I heard it the night everyone was helping get ready for the Hastings party and the night before the showing." Christie was warming to the story.

"So the last time we heard it, we dressed and took some flashlights outside," Sofia added.

Brett quailed at the thought but didn't interrupt the girls as they tag-teamed telling the story.

Christie nodded. "Right. Sofia's room is on the corner. The sounds echo kind of funny against the fence, and the lights flash like some kind of alien thing. But when you walk outside the fence, the sounds change. We walked all the way up the hill."

Brett interrupted and turned to Sofia. "To where the road turns, like in your painting?"

She nodded. "Once we got to the top of the hill, we could see the lights flashing like from a car and the noise sounded like an engine."

Christie shook her head. "Not like a car engine. More like a tractor."

Heavy equipment. Murphy's crew. Were they digging on Rafaela's property and Sofia had witnessed it?

Brett took a deep breath. If they were out there, that would be all the proof he needed to convince Rafaela.

"Did you see the lights tonight?"

"No. Not for the last two nights."

"OK. Get me your flashlights then you girls go on inside. I'm going to take a look."

"We want to go with you."

Brett glanced at Christie. She seemed ready for anything but Sofia stared at her, her eyes as wide as saucers.

"I'm not so sure your friend is as ready as you are to tackle the monster."

Christie glanced at Sofia and her shoulders

sagged. "It doesn't matter. You won't let us go anyway."

"You're right. I won't. All I'll do is take a look. If there's anything there, I promise I'll wake you and tell you all about it...right after I speak with Rafaela. She deserves to know first. Now scoot."

"I'll get the flashlights."

Christie took off at a run to the back of the house.

"Where's she going?"

Sofia smiled. "We've been crawling through my bedroom window. You don't think my mother would let us out on our own do you?"

Brett shook his head. "No and I don't think she'll be very happy with me for being in on your little secret either."

Sofia touched his arm. "But it won't be a secret for much longer. And it won't frighten me into nightmares anymore. My mother will appreciate *that* very much."

Brett smiled. Sometimes this fragile young lady was very wise for her age. He grasped her in a quick hug.

Christie returned with the flashlights.

Brett took the largest one from her and flipped it on. The bright light flashed clear across the yard. "Thanks. Now you two go back through that window. No more sneaking around in the dark."

Christie nodded.

As he walked away, Sofia called out to him. "Be careful. Please. Even if they're not monsters they're still not good men."

Brett waved in agreement and then skirted the dark edges of the lighted courtyard. The girls were right. Those men were dangerous. He would take a quick look around. If he saw any signs of digging or activity of any kind, he would head right back here, wake Rafaela, and rouse the whole house to tell his story. Then, they would do a thorough search in the daylight.

A full moon lit the road with a silvery glow. Fluffy, dark clouds dotted the night sky. Still, the stars seemed set in black velvet and twinkled brightly. The clear, brilliant air made the stars seem close enough to touch and illuminated everything, even creating shadows.

Brett left his headlights off and geared down as he made his way up the hill. All the while, he searched for movement or a flash of lights across the open plain. A long ridge rose along the base of the mesa, slowly climbing until, in the far distance, it ended in sandy cliffs with hollows.

A perfect cliff-dwelling location.

He slowed even more as he drove onto the dirt trail. His low profile car wasn't made for off-roading and he bottomed out several times even traveling at a snail's pace. *This car will get stuck, and I'll have to walk back to the ranch.* He looked in the rearview mirror, trying to judge the distance but there was no sign of the house, no lights even to point him in the right direction.

The going got rougher as the path climbed. Clouds drifted over the moon, and he had to pull over. The road completely disappeared as the light faded. He was about to climb out and walk when the slight breeze pushed away the cloud cover and silver light once again lit the way.

He wished he'd checked his odometer. Surely he'd crossed at least five miles. No wonder the sights and sounds were so distorted. By the time they reached

Sofia's bedroom window, they'd traveled over miles of desert hills and gullies.

Brett came to a wide area and a deep depression carved out by flash flooding. His car would never make it through. Shutting down the engine, he grabbed the flashlight and headed toward the cliff ridge.

The breeze picked up, sending clouds skittering across the sky and covering the moon. Ahead of him was a wide hollow set into the ridge. Probably ten feet deep and filled with shadows. The moonlight wavered. Was it a trick of the fluttering light or did the ground just below the ridge ripple?

Brett stopped and flipped the switch of his flashlight. The wind died as he flashed light along the area. The sand appeared darker, but nothing moved. The wavering must have been a trick of the cloudy light, because nothing moved at all.

The wind gusted, and Brett heard the distinct sound of cloth rippling in the breeze.

He flashed his light into the corner of the hollow. Sure enough, a sand-colored piece of canvas was attached to the roof of the hollow and pegged to the ground. It completely covered the corner, hiding what was behind.

Brett ran up the hill, kicking loose sand high in the air and almost tripping. When he finally reached the canvas, he pulled back the corner and looked inside. A small, yellow backhoe was parked in the corner. Shovels, picks, boxes, and crates were stacked against the dirt wall at the back.

A dig site. Squarely on Rancho de Silva property, almost within sight of the house. All this time, Pomeroy had been stealing from Rafaela and destroying a priceless archaeological site.

Brett had to get back. Had to stop Rafaela from selling to the low-down—

A slight rustling behind him sent him spinning around. Face-to-face with a burly man holding a crowbar high and ready to swing, Brett stumbled back and fell. He raised his arm to block the blow. Agony shot through his forearm. Then everything went black.

17

The low rumble of distant thunder woke Rafaela. *Great! On the day I'm going to sign over my home—the land my family has held for generations--the skies are going to open up and cry. That's all I need.*

Was it a sign? Was God weeping too?

Rolling over, she put such fanciful thoughts out of her mind and headed to the shower. Last night she'd been so tired, she'd dumped her clothes on the floor and left them. Now as she passed, the scent of smoke drifted up. As if she needed a reminder of what she had lost and was about to give away.

She made the water extra hot to wake her to drive those thoughts out of her head. She needed to be strong. To do what was right.

Halfway down the hall, she heard her mother humming in the kitchen. When her mother saw Rafaela, she threw her hands in the air. "Mija! I'm so glad you're finally awake. I have some great news to tell you, but you were so tired, I didn't have the heart to wake you."

Rafaela had news to tell her mother, too, but it wasn't so great. "First, coffee, Mama, then news. OK?"

Her mother poured her a large mug and set it front of her. But Mama couldn't wait until she'd had her first sip. "By the way, do you know where Brett is? Troy has been trying to reach him all morning. His cellphone must be dead."

Rafaela shook her head. "No. He left the gallery early." She didn't want to tell her mother why. Not just yet. She blew on her coffee and sipped.

"Troy will find him. He's headed into the gallery right now. Our news can't wait."

Rafaela paused. "What can't wait?"

Her mother clapped her hands together like a young girl. "The story about the fire reached the national news. Troy and Eliza's friends have been calling all morning. They want to help. All their offers gave Troy the idea for a benefit."

"A benefit?"

"A charity benefit. Alex will play. I'm sure my old dance troupe will come if I ask them. Isn't it a wonderful idea? One of Troy's friends even said he might commission a work from Emilio. God is so good!"

Stunned, Rafaela shook his head. "He may be good, but He's too late. I've agreed to sell the land to Tío Aaron."

"You did *what*?" Her mother's tone dropped to barely above a whisper. "Why would you do that after all we've done to keep it?"

"That's just the point, Mama. I didn't want to be like Papa. Year after year he put all of his energy and focus into his painting. Everything else came second. I don't want to be like that. If I sell, we'll have everything we need."

Lucia stared at her. "Not everything, Rafaela. Not faith and certainly not hope."

Rafaela gripped the mug in her hand. "What good is hope? Papa hoped that someday he'd make that big sale, that someone would discover him and proclaim him the next great Picasso. In the meantime, we stayed one step ahead of poverty."

"And now you hope money will make everything right. You are thinking so much like your father it frightens me."

Rafaela set the mug on the counter. "What are you talking about? I'm trying *not* to be like Papa. I'm giving up what I love to do what's right."

Her mother gave a shake of her head. "You're giving up for what you think is right. Have you asked God?"

Rafaela's lips parted. She wanted to say yes, but it would be a lie. She hadn't prayed. Hadn't asked God. She'd simply done what she thought was expected of her. Sacrificed for the ones she loved. But did God ask that sacrifice from her?

"Mija, listen to me. Your Papa was a good man. But somewhere along the line, he lost hope that a better future was waiting for him. He stopped taking chances, looking for the bright side. All he could see was the bad."

"Like me."

"Just like you. He didn't listen, didn't see how God was pointing the way. He trusted his own judgment more than God's. Then, when things went wrong, and of course they would go wrong, he lost his faith. He didn't believe God loved him enough to make things right."

"God *didn't* love him enough. He let him die." Bitterness filled Rafaela's words, and hot tears spilled down her cheeks.

Her mother rounded the corner of the countertop and wrapped her arms around Rafaela. All the tears and resentment she had held back for so long flowed out with her tears. Her mother held her, rocked her, and stroked her hair.

"It was your father's time, mija. But he could have left a happy man, content that he had lived a good life. He could have known he was going on to a better place, that he left us safe, with purpose and direction. But he didn't. He died sad and frightened for us."

She cupped Rafaela's cheeks and lifted her chin, brushed away the tears with her thumbs. "Don't let your father's only legacy be disillusionment, Rafaela. Learn what he could not. See God's hand in your life. Know that faith and hope conquer disillusionment."

Rafaela closed her eyes. "I lost hope long ago, and I think I've lost my faith, too," she whispered. "You're right. When I close my eyes, all I see is sadness. I see Angie's broken body lying on that gurney. It makes me cry that such a beautiful woman has lost her mind. I see glass on the ground, and I smell smoke. The charred pieces of Emilio's ruined work. Sofia's too-slender body. Where is hope, Mama? I don't see it."

"If that's all you see then you are not looking. Open your eyes, Rafaela."

Her mother's stern command startled her, and she opened her eyes.

Her mother gestured to the kitchen and the courtyard. "I see a home, a place of love built by generations who looked to the future and made a place for you and Sofia. Is that not God's hand?" She gave a little shake of her head. "We've always had help when we most needed it. We've never gone hungry. We've always had good doctors for Sofia. And speaking of your sister, have you looked at her lately, really looked?"

Her mother smiled. "She's happy, Rafaela. Maybe not completely healed, but happy, and that's the first step toward good health. Her laughter rings through this house." She squeezed Rafaela's arms. "I don't know how you can miss it. Everywhere I look, I find joy. I'm dancing and cooking. And we have new friends. We have—"

"Brett." Rafaela's word came out almost as a whisper.

Some of her mother's enthusiasm waned. "Yes, we have Brett. I'm not sure what's going on between you two, but I hope it's not serious. His presence in our lives is cause for great joy."

Fresh tears spilled down Rafaela's cheeks. "He tried to tell me, Mama. Called *me* a gift from God, and I didn't even respond." She took a deep breath and wiped the tears from her eyes. "I've been so foolish. I couldn't believe that I was meant to be happy. I even told Brett I didn't believe in happily-ever-after. I was afraid he would let me down, disappoint me. The first mistake he made, I used it as an excuse to condemn him."

Her mother shook her head. "You condemned yourself when you lost your faith in God."

"What do you mean?"

"You put your faith in yourself. You didn't believe—really believe—that God would pick you up and give you strength to go on, even if Brett let you down."

Rafaela straightened. "Is that what Papa did...allowed only the things he could handle into our lives?"

Her mother nodded. "I was guilty, too. I let it happen. I loved our home and being together. It was easier just to let your father handle what I thought were the 'details' of life. And by the time I realized what was happening, it was too late. Rafael was gone. Only then did I realize how many doors God had opened for us, how many opportunities we missed simply because Rafael was afraid to step through those open doors." Reaching across the space, she stroked Rafaela's hair once again. "And it fell to you, mija, to pick up the pieces. Your sister became so ill; all I could do was take care of her."

Rafaela's head hung. "I think I was angry with God for taking Papa. Maybe that's when I stopped believing in things bigger than me, like His power and a love He ordained for me." She shook her head. "I've been so wrong. What will I do?"

Reaching across the counter, her mother pulled a tissue from a box and handed it to her. "Well, first thing, you find Brett and tell him what you just told me."

Rafaela glanced at the clock. "No, the first thing I have to do is call Tío Aaron. I'm supposed to be at his office in twenty minutes to sign the papers."

"I'll call Aaron. I have a few things to say to him anyway."

Rafaela hugged her mother. "Thanks, Mama. I love you."

Her mother returned the hug, squeezing hard. "Now get going. I'm sure Brett's at the gallery."

Rafaela grabbed her purse and hurried to her truck. She pulled onto the highway, her foot heavy on the gas. She was halfway to town when her cellphone rang. She pulled over to the side of the road and answered her mother's call.

"I can't reach Aaron. He's not answering his phone and there's no one at the office either."

"That's OK. He's probably with a client. But we

agreed to meet, so he'll be at the office soon. I'll swing by on my way to the gallery and talk to him. Thanks." She'd barely hung up when she received a text from Aaron.

Running late at a meeting. Can you meet me at this address?

The address was one she didn't recognize and appeared to be out of her way. But she owed Tío a decent explanation.

She touched the highlighted address. Her GPS clicked on. Pulling back onto the road, she followed the program's verbal directions.

~*~

Rafaela drove to the outskirts of town. The sky was dark and ominous. Clouds gathered for a downpour. She hoped to find the meeting place and be inside before the deluge.

The address Tío had sent her was in an industrial area. Large complexes and huge metal buildings lined the road. Warehouses situated in open yards appeared empty.

A drizzle started just as Rafaela pulled into a fenced complex. The massive metal building bore a sign that read *Murphy's Construction*. She parked in front and sat for a moment, watching the raindrops collect on her windshield.

Not far away, a group of men huddled beneath a metal awning, trying to avoid the rain.

Rafaela hoped to avoid it, too. She hopped out of the truck, still watching the huddled group of men. No one came forward to give her directions.

Was it her imagination, or did they seem slightly

hostile? They were almost glaring, leaning against the awning supports, hands in their pockets and scowls on their faces.

They made her a little nervous just standing there watching, until she recognized a familiar face. A friend of Emilio and his cousins stood near the front. Bert. She started to wave as he turned and jogged across the parking lot to his car.

Her hand fell to her side. Obviously she was mistaken. It couldn't have been Bert.

The rain began to fall in earnest. Ducking her head, she dashed for the front door of the warehouse.

The massive building was dark. Light fell from the door into the black area, lighting a few nearby crates but little else.

"Tío?"

Her voice sounded small in the large building, especially as the rain beat against the metal roof with a steady pounding.

She spotted an enclosed office off to the side. Blinds covered all the windows, but light peeked out beneath. Closing the door behind her, she walked across the cement floor. The sound of her heels disappeared in the staccato rain. She knocked on the door.

"Come in, "Tío Aaron called out.

She couldn't believe how relieved she was to hear his voice. Grasping the handle, she twisted it quickly and stepped inside.

Tío sat at a big desk covered in papers. A desk lamp pointed down, pinpointing a stack of documents.

"Rafaela, I'm glad you finally made it." His expression was taut. Nothing in his features seemed glad. In fact, he seemed nervous.

A prickling started at the back of her neck. "I wasn't sure I was going to make it. This is an odd place to meet, Tío."

"I had a meeting with Mr. Murphy that ran late. It seemed best to have you come here rather than wait for me at the office."

The prickling crawled down her arms and raised into goose-bumps. "I think I would rather have waited at your office."

He rose. "Yes, it's a foul day to be out and about. Let's get this over with so you can get home."

He gestured for her to come forward. Something in his gaze—an intensity or anger, she couldn't tell which—made her hesitate. She didn't want to go closer. She wanted to turn and leave. "Actually, Tío, I need to talk to you. I'm sorry. I know you've gone to a lot of trouble, but I've changed my mind. I don't want to sell."

Her uncle straightened to his full height. The desk lamp created strange shadows, making him seem taller. Bigger. More frightening.

Ridiculous. Her imagination was playing havoc with her senses. This was Tío Aaron.

"You're right." His tone deepened, and yes, it held a strong vein of anger.

Maybe it wasn't her imagination.

"I have gone to a lot of trouble, over and over again. I've always been there for you, pulling you out of the fire, helping when no one else would."

Rafaela swallowed. "Yes, Tío, and I love you for it. We all do. But if I sell, all of our work will have been for nothing. I can't sell, not when things are just getting better. It's not the time to sell."

"Now *is* the time to sell." He pounded the desk

with his fist and Rafaela jumped back, startled.

He pressed his fists on the firm surface and drew a deep breath. "Sofia needs help. And your mother...hasn't she suffered enough?"

Rafaela paused. Her own exact words.

But were they really? How many times had Tío said this to her? Over and over again until it became a recording in her head. Until she believed they were her own words. Her thoughts.

"No." She shook her head slowly. "She's not suffering. She's the one who told me to come here. She said you would understand."

With his gaze still lowered, he gave a negative shake. "Then don't do it for her. Do it for me. I need this, Rafaela. I've run out of time." His sounded hurt, desperate.

"I don't understand. Time for what? Are you in financial trouble, Tío?"

"Don't ask. Please, just sign the papers." He looked up and his gaze burned.

"I can't. Not like this. Not unless I understand."

"Rafaela, I'm begging you. Sign them now." He pinned her beneath a desperate, tortured gaze.

She needed to leave, to get out. She backed up, slowly, one step at a time.

The door behind her slammed open. A large man she didn't recognize lunged through and grabbed her. "I told you she wouldn't do it." The man twisted her arm and she cried out.

"Take it easy, Murphy. I told you not to hurt her."

"Tío! Who is this man? Tell him to let me go."

Her uncle shook his head. "I begged you, Rafaela. Begged you. Now I have no other choice." Tío leaned over the desk and hung his head.

The burly man twisted her arm and leaned close, his hot breath in her face. "Now we do it my way."

He dragged her out the door. As soon as they stepped into the large warehouse, Rafaela screamed. "Help! Help me!"

Her voice was pounded out by the rain on the metal roof.

The man twisted her arm tighter. "Don't waste your time. Those are my men out there. They know better than to interfere."

He pushed her ahead of him. Rafaela struggled against his grip, fearful she might trip and fall as he pushed her through the darkened building. Pausing by a wall, he flipped a switch. Light flooded the room and Rafaela gasped.

In the center of the workroom, Brett was precariously perched on one step of a tall ladder. His hands were tied behind his back. He had a bloodied bruise on the side of his head and appeared to be dazed as he swayed back and forth on the slender step.

Ice ran through her veins. A rope wrapped around his neck was looped over a metal rafter and tied to another support. One wrong move or dizzy spell and he would hang.

"Brett!" She lunged forward but the burly man pulled her back against him.

"That's right. We have your boyfriend. Now either you sign that paper or I kick that ladder right out from under him."

Rafaela struggled, fighting helplessly against his considerable strength.

"Who *are* you? *Why* do you want my land?"

Aaron came out of the office and stood in front of them.

"Why, Tío? Why are you doing this?"

He shook his head. "The village, Rafaela. The Chaco village. They all talked about it and fantasized over it but your father refused to look. I found it. Just beneath the ridge. A whole village just waiting to be uncovered."

"Chaco artifacts? You're doing this for money?" She stared at him, shock sweeping through her.

He smiled. "That's what your father thought, too. But it was never about the money. Not for me."

The man behind her grunted. "That didn't stop you from taking your share of what we sold on the black market."

Aaron glared at him.

Understanding began to filter through Rafaela. "You've been selling artifacts?"

Her uncle didn't answer but his partner laughed. Something cold hardened inside Rafaela.

"You made the noises in the night? You knew all the time and didn't try to help Sofia?" She stared at Aaron, the man her family had thought they knew so well, and shook her head. "Did you ever really care about us or was it always an act?"

"I cared." Aaron spun in disgust. "Too much. I wanted to be one of you, the de Silvas, the Hastingses, and the Luceros. I wanted so badly to belong, but I was never really one of the 'inner circle' because I didn't know about the village. They wouldn't tell me the location. They thought I couldn't be trusted with the secret."

"They were obviously right." Rafaela spat out.

"True. But now I have my own secret. I've seen the village, touched the sandals and arrowheads they only dreamed about. All they did was talk about those things buried in the ground. They weren't brave enough to actually look for them. I did it. I found the stuff without their help. I dug them up, touched them, kept them in my home, and then I sold them. I have the control, and I'm the one with the best kept secret."

Murphy twisted her arm. "That's enough talking. Sign the papers or I'll pull that ladder away and you can watch your boyfriend choke to death."

Hot tears flooded her eyes, and she sagged against the man. Slowly, she shook her head. "You won't let us live even if I do sign. You can't. You want the land so you can make all of your sales legal. If I'm alive, that won't happen."

Murphy cursed. Swinging her around, he slapped her hard across the face. Rafaela went flying several feet away. She fell hard, her head spinning. Wild thoughts danced through her mind. This was how her life was going to end. No happy ending for her or for Brett. *No! Not this way. God wants me to live, to be happy.* She gathered her reeling senses and looked up.

Murphy pulled a gun out of the back of his pants and aimed at her.

Rafaela screamed. "Tío!"

Aaron Pomeroy stepped forward and shoved the gun upwards. The blast echoed and reechoed in the metal building.

"I told you, not while I'm here," he shouted.

His partner spun and leaned into his face. "What difference does it make if you see it or not? It will happen and your hands are just as bloody as mine."

"I told you, I don't want to see it."

Rafaela saw her opportunity. Lunging to her feet, she ran straight ahead. Catching Murphy sideways, she used all her strength to shove him into her uncle.

Both men fell backwards. She ran for the door, expecting any minute to feel a bullet in her back.

The front door opened and Murphy's workers came running through.

"Police! There are police outside."

The men ran toward the back, passing a spinning Murphy. Two policemen knelt in a puddle just outside the front door, guns drawn and pointed inside.

Rafaela heard an engine revving over the sound of the rain, louder and louder. A huge yellow bulldozer crashed through the walls with the bending and screeching of metal. It plowed straight through, destroying everything in its path.

Bert. He must have called the police and now sat in the driver's seat of the caterpillar. More police climbed through the opening he'd created in the wall.

Tío Aaron turned and ran out the back.

Murphy cursed. He glared at Rafaela for what seemed like an eternity.

In that moment, she realized what he was going to do. He intended to get back at her through Brett. She ran toward the ladder, determined to get there first.

Murphy was ahead of her. She'd never reach Brett before the awful man pulled the ladder from beneath his feet.

But Bert would. He never slowed or stopped the bulldozer. Out of the corner of her gaze, she saw him shift gears, and the front bucket began to rise.

Murphy and Bert reached Brett at the same time. Murphy jerked the ladder to the side, turned, and ran toward the back of the building.

Brett cried out as his feet met open air.

The bucket caught him, scooping him inside and cradling him like a baby.

The bulldozer kept going until it tipped over the ladder. It fell slowly but steadily right into Murphy's back. He tumbled forward hard, face first. The gun skittered into the dark recesses of the building. A policeman jumped on Murphy's back and pinned him with a knee.

Rafaela never stopped running. Even as Bert pulled the bulldozer to a stop and stood in the seat, she grabbed the notches of the huge tires and climbed. The bucket was within reach. She latched onto it, hooked a leg over and slid inside.

Brett lay on his side, struggling to use his bound hands to help him rise. Trembling, she loosened the knot of rope around his neck and threw it over the side. Then she looped her arms around him and pulled him close.

"Rafaela, I thought for sure—"

"Shh…" She stroked his hair away from the raw, bleeding wound on the side of his head. "Don't say it," she whispered. "I never doubted. I knew God wouldn't let it end that way. He spent too much time trying to teach me a lesson."

"What lesson?"

"This one." She kissed him long and hard, even as Bert lowered the bucket to the ground and tilted them out.

The surrounding police laughed as Brett and Rafaela rolled free, still clasped together.

"Look at this," one of the policemen called out. "The perps are caught. The hostages are safe, and not a shot's been fired. This is a 'for real' happy ending."

Rafaela kissed Brett again as the crowd around them clapped.

18

Rafaela insisted Brett follow doctor's orders and take a few weeks to recuperate from the concussion he suffered at Jay Murphy's hands. He complied with thinly veiled impatience while she planned the charity benefit.

With Alex and Troy's help, the event became another highlight of Santa Fe's social season and once again, the de Silva Gallery made the national headline news.

Per Alex's request, Rafaela's mother danced while he played La Guitarra. He said the legend of the lost lovers could now be laid to rest and La Guitarra was at peace.

Her mother's performance was extraordinary. She positively glowed.

Daniel Fallon clearly agreed, as he spent the entire night by her side.

Sofia was able to miss a few days of school to attend and managed the crowds and the excitement without a problem. Of course, having her best friend, Christie, with her for encouragement helped.

Brett brought the evening to an end in the most perfect way. He bent down on one knee and proposed to Rafaela in front of the entire crowd.

"I want a short engagement," Brett whispered in her ear as they danced on the plaza grass, moving to the slow strains of the band hired for the event.

"I couldn't agree more." She wrapped her arms around his neck.

"If we didn't have all this business to take care of, I'd marry you next week."

"We could elope."

He shook his head, and a secretive smile slipped over his lips. "I have something very special in mind."

No matter how many ways she teased and asked, he wouldn't reveal his plan.

"I can't wait."

"You'll have to."

"Darn business."

"You don't feel that way and you know it."

She didn't. The village Aaron had discovered was now Rafaela's business, and no matter how hard she tried, she could no longer bring herself to call him Tío.

Aaron and his cohorts were in jail awaiting trial for attempted murder. After that trial, they'd face charges in a Federal court for theft and the illegal sale of protected artifacts.

In an ironic twist, Aaron made Rafaela's mother the manager of his estate while he was serving what would be a lifetime sentence. The position proved a substantial monthly income. In addition, she was the beneficiary in his will. Overnight, her mother became a wealthy woman.

Rafaela never understood if Aaron did it to try to atone, or simply because he trusted no one else. No matter what his reasoning, his actions testified to his disturbing and convoluted mental and emotional state.

Aaron and Murphy had uncovered but a small portion of a substantial Chaco village located beneath the shelter of the mesa's ridge.

The University of New Mexico offered to excavate

the site in a scholarly and respectful manner and paid Rafaela a substantial sum for the rights.

She'd agreed only after consulting with the Pueblo tribes. They established a non-profit organization and created a museum to manage the artifacts with most of the profits returning to the tribes. The grandson of Ruben Lucero served as the representative of the nineteen tribes. He worked closely with Brett who was the chair and director of the non-profit.

"I've been training all my life for this," he said when Rafaela asked him to take the position. "No one would do a better job."

Business was booming. With all the additional publicity, they continued to have visitors anxious to see the gallery surrounded by so much drama. Between the visitors and the constant stream of curiosity seekers, Rafaela didn't know whether to consider the attention a blessing or a curse. She was so busy that she had to recruit Emilio for help.

The constant stream of onlookers gave her an idea. By the time the repairs were almost complete, she proposed an addition. She wanted them to add a permanent workshop in the front for Emilio so he could work on his craft for a portion of the day. Passersby could watch and ask questions and generate interest. She even suggested that Emilio ask some of his relatives to come as visiting artists. Emilio loved the idea but expressed concerned about the expense of the construction.

"That's not even an issue," Rafaela assured him. "The 'artist in residence' will generate so much publicity, it will more than pay for itself. Besides," she said nudging him in the arm. "I am engaged, soon to be married. How else are you going to work and take care of the gallery when I stay home to have my babies?"

"Babies? I'll be an uncle?" His dazed expression ended his concerns about finances and started a whole set of new ones.

The wedding preparations were simple. Not nearly as lavish as the celebration Rafaela and Brett attended earlier in the fall. The wedding of Lara Fallon and Alexander Summers made the national society columns.

Daniel Fallon spared no expense to see his only daughter wed to the man she loved.

Brett, Rafaela, and her family attended, amongst a group of notables which included a few Spanish dignitaries.

For all the magnificent decorations and incredible food, Lara Fallon's dress was exquisitely simple—a long, single sheath that dipped low in the back and trailed behind her. She looked amazing.

Rafaela cried when she saw her and hoped she would look as beautiful at her wedding.

Afterwards, their own wedding plans kicked into gear.

Brett hired Bert to help him with some things at the rancho.

Rafaela watched in amazement as Brett opened a wall at the back of the living room and put in new French doors, creating another courtyard at the back of the house. He added saltillo tiles and a covered awning.

She thought he was crazy when he tore down the back fence he'd so recently repaired...until she saw the sun setting behind the distant hills.

When her wedding day finally arrived, she

stepped onto the purple bougainvillea-draped, Spanish-styled gazebo, and thanked God once again for the brilliant, thoughtful man she was about to marry.

She wore a flaring flamenco-style white dress, off the shoulders, ruffled at the knees and flowing in the back with yards of antique lace. She'd pulled her hair back with a mother-of-pearl mantilla and a lace veil that had been worn by her grandmother. Delicate, cascading red roses fell over her hands.

Brett stood beside her.

The distant mountains spread before them in a stunning vista as the sun dipped behind the purple-hued hills. The beautiful Santa Fe sky, laced with wispy clouds, vivid pinks and gentle mauves, turned to lilac as they made their vows.

Brett said his first.

Then the reverend posed his question to Rafaela. "Do you take this man to be your lawfully wedded husband?"

"I do and I promise to always remember Psalm 37:4 'Take delight in the Lord and He will give you the desires of your heart.'"

The pastor was startled by her little unrehearsed addition but she had no doubt that Brett understood. It was her vow to honor God's promise for them, to always believe and have hope.

Not waiting for the reverend's instructions, Brett swept Rafaela into his arms and sealed her vow with a kiss.

Thank you

We appreciate you reading this White Rose Publishing title. For other inspirational stories, please visit our on-line bookstore at www.pelicanbookgroup.com.

For questions or more information, contact us at customer@pelicanbookgroup.com.

White Rose Publishing
Where Faith is the Cornerstone of Love™
an imprint of Pelican Ventures Book Group
www.PelicanBookGroup.com

Connect with Us
www.facebook.com/Pelicanbookgroup
www.twitter.com/pelicanbookgrp

To receive news and specials, subscribe to our bulletin
http://pelink.us/bulletin

May God's glory shine through
this inspirational work of fiction.

AMDG

Free Book Offer

We're looking for booklovers like you to partner with us! Join our team of influencers today and receive at least one free eBook per month. Maybe more!

For more information
Visit http://pelicanbookgroup.com/booklovers
or e-mail
booklovers@pelicanbookgroup.com